The Mysteriou

Or, The Foundling. A Story for Boys and Girls

Anonymous

Alpha Editions

This edition published in 2024

ISBN : 9789361473012

Design and Setting By
Alpha Editions
www.alphaedis.com
Email - info@alphaedis.com

Contents

CHAPTER I.

THE UNWELCOME DISCOVERY.

"They are wondrous merry to-night in the upper inn," said Hicup (the landlord of the one lower down the village) to his wife, who was turning over the leaves of the almanac. He sulkily threw his cap off his head, and flung himself into an easy-chair.--"All the windows are lighted up in the principal room, and there is no end to the strumming of fiddles; the beer-room is swarming with customers and strangers, whose conveyances are standing before the door as a show to torment me. Why does no one ever come our way now? Although the wooden arm holding the beer-can stretches itself out ever so far, inviting the travellers to come in, not an individual enters the door, not a turn do we get!--Is it any wonder, then, if the beer in the cellar turns sour, and that the last customer who found his way here by chance, was frightened away by it? But this is always the way in the world,--where pigeons are, there pigeons fly."

"The people must be bewitched," said Dame Hicup, in a stammering voice.

Hicup looked attentively at his wife, and then at the brandy bottle, which stood near her in a corner cupboard.

"So you have been at the brandy again, you old witch, and half-emptied the bottle!" said our host in a rage, seizing his stick. "Wait, I will give you"----. A loud knocking at the window-shutter interrupted both the sentence and the intended castigation.

"Who's there?" he bawled out.

"A poor woman, who begs a lodging for the night," was the answer.

"A poor woman," continued Hicup sullenly. "Such guests are always to be had; you had better go up to the other inn, you will be more comfortable there than with us."

Dame Hicup, to whom this interruption was most opportune, having a due regard for her bones, became, all of a sudden, compassionate. "He who sends the poor from his door," she began, "to him Heaven will not send the rich;" and, without waiting for the assent of her husband, she stepped across the room, and opened the door. A woman, poorly clad, with a large handkerchief hanging behind her head, and a basket on her back, stood before her.

"Come in, come in," said Dame Hicup invitingly, bringing her into the room.

"Have you a passport?" gruffly demanded the landlord.

"Yes; here it is;" and the woman drew from her pocket a piece of folded paper, which she handed to the master of the inn, who, without looking at it, said, "Where are you going?"

"To Neiderhaslich."

"What's your occupation? What are you carrying?"

"I deal in crockery and stoneware; therefore I must take care, and put down my basket gently."

"Umph! umph!" growled Hicup; then, turning to his wife, he muttered in a tolerably audible voice, "Do you mean to give the woman a bed in the low room? It is not the first time that such gentry have packed up all they could get, and gone off during the night, finding their way out by the window."

The stranger had heard every word; but far from seeming offended, merely said, "You need not put straw in the room for me, as any corner in an out-house, or in a stable, will do well enough."

"All the stalls are empty, the more's the pity," replied Dame Hicup; "so if you prefer being there,"----

"Oh! yes," eagerly interrupted the traveller, going to lift up her basket again.

"Leave that where it is," said the suspicious Hicup, who saw in it security for the reckoning; "it will be safer here, and more readily lifted on again, than in the stable."

"Could we not make a bargain?" asked the landlady insinuatingly; "such brittle goods are always wanted."

"No, no," replied the stranger hastily; "everything in the basket is bespoke, and carefully packed up; I would lose my custom were I to open it. Perhaps another time"----

"Oh! there is no haste," answered Dame Hicup; "the thought only happened to come into my head."

The stranger quickly swallowed some liquid, took a piece of bread in her hand, and, under the pretext of being very tired, went away, accompanied by the hostess, who wished to show her where she was to sleep.

Our host, meanwhile, was still sitting in his arm-chair, thinking with envy of his rival, the landlord of the upper inn. The moment his wife came back, she made her way straight to the basket, with the intention of having a peep at its contents in spite of its cover. The threatening voice, however, of her husband defeated her purpose. "Hands off, there! I see you are dying with curiosity to know what is in the basket; but, as a punishment for your brandy-drinking, you shall not get leave to touch it; and this is a far less punishment than you deserve."

In a very discontented mood, but dreading the anger of her husband, Dame Hicup sat down again at the table. All was so quiet, that gradually the eyes of both closed, and, not being disturbed with much light, as the candle was burnt out, they fell asleep.

Suddenly Dame Hicup started up,--"Do you want anything?" she asked.

"No," answered her partner, angry at being awakened; "but, yes, I would like to be the landlord of the inn up there."

After these few words, all was quiet again, until a kind of creaking noise was heard, and a half-suppressed cry struck their ears; at which Hicup, terrified, sprang from his chair. "Wife! wife!" he shouted, shaking the Dame; "do you not hear?--thieves are breaking in!"

No thieves broke in, but the voices of two children broke out into a cry, and, at the same time, the basket creaked and moved. With eyes wide open, the angry landlord stared at the mysterious basket. His wife, on whose mind the truth seemed to flash, hastily pulled away the cover, and saw, to her no small dismay, the heads of two children lying close together. She clasped her hands in terror, while her husband muttered to himself,--"Fine earthenware indeed! Out of such clay are we all made."

"Come! come!" quickly cried his wife, dragging him after her; "a thought strikes me!" It struck the good man too, when they had sought the stable in vain for the owner of the basket. Hicup again wished to make use of his stick to put his wife in remembrance that she had brought the vagabond into the house; but Dame Hicup retorted, throwing the blame on her husband, who, by preventing her looking into the basket, had given the woman time to escape. Our hostess examined minutely the foundlings and their cradle, and our host gave vent to his wrath in every variety of words.

"Now, truly, we have got all at once precious guests!" he said, laughing scornfully. "Fine food this for the village gossips! But he who has the misfortune, need not concern himself about the joking. Wife, if you don't get rid instantly of the squalling brats, you shall pay dearly for it. We have scarce bread enough for ourselves, and are we to divide it with cast-away infants? Take them up to the landlord at the other end of the village, from whose table plenty crumbs fall to keep them. It is a good thing that we have neither servant-maid nor boy in the house to carry tales."

By this time, Dame Hicup had lifted the children out of the basket, and again, by dint of hushing, made them quiet. They fixed their eyes on their new nurse, and stretched out their little arms in the air. They were both boys, of the same size, remarkably alike, and about seven or eight months old.

"They are twins," said Dame Hicup with the greatest certainty; "as for their mother, the woman who left them is too old, and their linen too fine."

"Would it were coarse as hemp!" interrupted the wrathful landlord, "to hang the vagrant. Make haste, I tell you, and free the house of these urchins; put some brandy into their milk, that they may sleep soundly, and then make the landlord of the upper inn a present of them."

The Dame did as she was bid, without making the slightest attempt to induce her husband to keep the deserted infants. She mixed the brandy with the milk, which the children greedily swallowed, and soon after fell asleep.

With one small burden under each arm, the mistress of the inn left her house late in the night. When she returned with empty hands in about half-an-hour, her husband, who was anxiously waiting, cried out to her in great glee,--"So you have really got rid of them! tell me how."

"There were too many people in the inn for me to venture within the door," answered his wife; "but at the outside of the entrance a travelling carriage was standing, whose driver had gone seemingly into the beer-room to get a glass of something. I heard a loud snoring from some one in the back seat; but in the front there was nothing but parcels and packages; so I laid the one youngster softly down on the top of them, and the other I slipped into a horse's manger which was close to the door of the inn."

"Thank our stars!" said worthy Master Hicup, "that we have escaped at the expense of only a good fright."

CHAPTER II.

THE VILLAGE MUSICIAN.

It was already far past midnight, and still the dance in the salle in the upper inn had not ceased. Never had the dancers been more indefatigable at their hardest work than they were now, as they panted for breath, and glowed with heat. More and more wearied became the musicians, as they wetted their parched throats alternately with beer and brandy.

"Let us have the grandfather's dance for a finish!" cried the boldest dancer-- one who was always last at work, and therefore last at the dance--to the young girls, who were preparing to go away. "Holloa! you fiddlers, play us something sprightly, and don't spare either your breadth or your bones. The grandfather's dance! do you hear?" and seizing the hand of his partner, he began to sing in a loud voice,

"When our grandsire took our granddame home,

The lady was bride, and he bridegroom."

The player of the clarionet blew until his thin cheeks were puffed out like a drum, and his eyes almost started out of their sockets. The violin-player showed equal zeal in the use of his bow; while the violincello sounded mightily; and the tones of the flute pierced through bones and marrow. When the dance was finished, its hero, wiping the dew from his forehead, addressed his companions in amusement, saying, "All's well that ends well;" and drinking a glass of cold beer, he left the inn, accompanied by the whole party, who went shouting and laughing through the silent village, disturbing the quiet of its inhabitants.

"Young blood is warm," said the landlord, as he heard the noise, and was extinguishing the lights in the salle.

A traveller, who had been prevented by the uproar of the dancers and the sound of music from going to bed, heard the remark of the landlord, and replied, with asperity, "Certainly a noble way of exercising youthful spirits to destroy the night's rest of industrious peasants, to waste the earnings of honest parents, and to ruin their own health. Such a dancing-room is a chapel of Satan, and the landlord and the musicians are the priests."

Had the speaker been a common person, assuredly the landlord would have poured out his wrath on him. He contented himself, however, by saying to the musicians, when the stranger had left, "That fellow must surely be a

Methodist, a Quaker, or a Herrnhuter! Were all the world of his way of thinking, we should soon be ruined."

The musicians nodded their assent to this remark; and after dividing their gains, they likewise left the house.

It was quite dark, therefore no wonder that the tired and not perfectly sober band had great difficulty in finding their way down the flight of steps which led from the house to the street. The violincellist missed his footing, and rolled from the top to the bottom of the stairs. A crashing noise announced his arrival on the ground, and also the fate of the instrument.

"So the violincello is in the mud!" cried the clarionet-player, with the utmost stoical indifference, from the top of the stairs.

"Not at all; quite the reverse!" replied the prostrate fiddler, with equal calmness; "the mud is in the violincello." He raised himself up from the instrument, which had so broken his fall, that he felt not much the worse of it; and amidst jokes and laughter, the damage done to the violincello was examined, and was found to be considerable, as the back part of it was entirely broken to pieces.

"I have heard my father say," began the flute-player, in a tone of condolence, "that the more a violincello was glued together, the finer were its tones."

At this moment sounds were heard, not exactly like the tones of a violin, but rather resembling those of an oboe. The artists, amazed, looked round for their invisible companion, but saw nothing. Again the sound was heard, and more distinctly. It was the voice of a crying child, that seemed to come from a manger close beside them. As soon as the musicians had satisfied themselves, by seeing as well as hearing, with the exception of the bassist, they all took to flight.

"I have children enough to feed," thought the flute-player.

"And I, I have scarcely bread for myself," said the player on the clarionet.

"My wife would scratch out my eyes," ejaculated the violin-player, "were I to bring a foundling into the house."

Kummas, the violincellist, who had fallen down the stairs, felt a spark of pity for the poor child, whose bitter cries broke the stillness of the night. He went up the steps again, in order to acquaint the landlord with what had been found, and to induce him to take the infant under his care.

But he found the house-door firmly locked, and all his knocking and calling remained unanswered. This deafness, however, of the master of the inn had nothing to do with hard-heartedness, as he knew not of the poor child, whose cold cradle was becoming every moment more uncomfortable.

Sunk in profound meditation, the village musician now stood before the screaming infant. A complete revolution seemed to be taking place in his mind,--one of those sudden, incomprehensible, and unlooked for changes which sometimes passes over the spirit of man. He had seen, with utter indifference, hundreds of young blooming creatures led into much evil by the wild excess of dancing; indeed, helped them on by his music, without his conscience ever having reproached him. Beer and brandy were his gods. Them he had worshipped; and his memory could not call up a single action that he had done in accordance with the will of his Creator. But the hard crust of his heart now gave way. Feelings came over him like those with which, as a child, he had regarded pictures of the manger where his Saviour lay cradled, given him by his pious parents at the good Christmas time, to keep him in remembrance of the sacred event. Now there lay before him, in such a manger, a helpless infant, stretching out its little arms towards him. Kummas remembered the long forgotten words of the Lord Jesus, "Whoso shall receive one such little child in my name, receiveth me." He took up the infant, pressed it tenderly to his heart, spoke to it caressingly, silently promising never to leave it, or forsake it. Already he received the reward of his first good deed. An undescribable joy, such as the most intoxicating draught had never caused, filled his whole soul, and made everything appear brighter in his eyes. Softer blew the night air on his burning face. More beautiful shone the silver stars; and even the voice of the village watchman appeared melodious, as he greeted the coming day with the words,

"Jesus' goodness has no end,

It is every morning new!"

The foundling appeared to be neither bad tempered, nor accustomed to very careful nursing. Quicker than Kummas hoped, it became quiet, and fell asleep. He remembered his broken violincello, and, gently as possible, he laid the little sleeper in the musical cradle, carried it carefully, and began in this fashion his pilgrimage to the next village, and to his miserable cottage, into which he brought his little clarionet, as he sportingly called the child, in safety. Only once had he found it necessary, before day-break, to set the new-fashioned cradle in motion, and to sing, "Hush! hush!"

CHAPTER III.

THE NEW-FASHIONED NURSE.

"Have you not made a mistake, neighbour?" asked Anne Maria, the peasant into whose house Kummas had gone very early in the morning. "The tavern is lower down the village, and I keep no brandy."

For the first time for many years, Kummas felt his face grow red. "I wish to buy a can of milk," he replied.

"Milk!" exclaimed the peasant, astonished. "This must be before your end! I have certainly heard that milk-drinkers may become brandy-drinkers; but never the reverse."

Kummas patiently endured the rebuke of the good woman, as a punishment for his former mode of life. He then continued, "If you could give me the milk new from the cow, and still warm, I would like it better. I have got a guest. The stork last night brought me a little child; and, as you have children, I wish you to tell me how it must be treated and nursed."

"Go away!" said the woman angrily; "I have no time for your foolish jests."

"Well!" answered Kummas, "if you will not believe my words, you will, perhaps, believe your own eyes."

It may be imagined how great was the astonishment of the peasant, when, in a few minutes, Kummas returned with the infant in his arms. When her surprise at the unexpected appearance had somewhat abated, she said to Kummas, at the same time laying her hand on his shoulder, "Neighbour, you are really better than I gave you credit for, and are an honest man. That is a splendid child. God bless it! Stout and strong as a young lion. Now he opens his pretty blue eyes. So you would like something to drink, my fine fellow? Eh! Haste, Hannah, and bring us some milk from the cow," she said, turning to a young girl who was beside her; "and now, let me see if you are rightly dressed. There, neighbour, hold the young rascal, until I bring something else to put on him. He is so strong that you may hold him upright already."

Kummas knew not how to hold the half-naked child; and from pure terror, lest he might hurt it, allowed it almost to fall out of his arms. He paid particular attention to what the peasant did as she dressed it again, and gave it the warm milk, which it seemed to like very much.

"And how sensible it is!" began again the good woman. "Does it not drink out of the cup just like one of ourselves? Hark ye, neighbour, you must just leave the youngster with me."

"No! no!" replied Kummas most decidedly.

"I will give you a bottle of brandy for him," again said the peasant.

"I will not give him for a whole cask!" exclaimed the musician.

"Indeed! that from you says much. But what will come of the child when you go out to play at night?" asked the kind woman.

"I do not mean to play any longer," answered Kummas.

"Are you in earnest?" said Anne Maria. "If so, heaven be praised! for truly the beer-fiddling is a wretched sort of life,--a way of living that makes weak legs and red faces. I have seen all such persons die in poverty and misery; for they almost all took to brandy drinking; and you were far on the road yourself."

Once more Kummas felt ashamed at the truthful words of his neighbour, who kindly, however, added, "Don't take amiss what I say. I mean well to you. Every morning I will give you milk for the foundling, and will look after its clothes. And I have nothing to say against your playing at a respectable marriage, or on a feast-day, when I will take good care of your youngster in your absence. But what do you call him?"

"He has no doubt been baptised," answered Kummas; "however, as I know not his right name, I will just call him Christlieb Fundus."

Had the poor child been forcibly thrust upon the village in which Kummas lived for maintenance, in all likelihood the inhabitants would have resisted doing anything for it. As the case stood, it was quite the reverse. A blessing seemed to have come along with the foundling. Everybody was curious to see the new-fashioned cradle; and no one came empty-handed; so that Kummas saw himself in possession of different articles of food, clothes for the child, and other things,--all unlooked for, and most unexpected; while he himself rose in the estimation of the villagers,--an advantage which formerly he had neither known nor prized.

Some weeks had passed away, when one morning Kummas received a visit from one of his former companions, in the shape of Schubert, the flute-player.

The interior of the small apartment presented to the visitor, at his entrance, a singular enough appearance. His eye fell first on the well-known large violin, which, still without its back, had its two sides supported by rounded pieces of wood,--such as cradles usually have. On the soft bedding, which filled the hollow space, lay a sleeping infant, whose rosy cheeks told of health and plenty. A few steps from this sat Kummas at a low table, which was covered with wire, small pieces of wood, and various kinds of implements. On the floor were scattered about sauce-pans, pots, and all sorts of broken earthenware, waiting to be mended by the hands of the late musician, who, at that moment, was occupied repairing an old bird-cage. A string was fastened to his right foot, the other end of which, being attached to the violincello-cradle, served as a means for setting it in motion whenever the little sleeper showed symptoms of restlessness.

"It is true, then, what I heard, but would not believe!" exclaimed Schubert, in a scornful voice. "So you have become an old woman!--a nurse! Are you mad, or"----

"I wish you good morning," said Kummas coolly, thus reminding his comrade of the omitted salutation. "You ask how I am? and I answer quite well. Never was better in my life."

"That shows me you are a fool!" replied Schubert. "Have I not children myself; and do I not know how I am tormented at nights by their squalling and screaming, not to speak of the thousand things my wife has to do for them?"

"It is true," said Kummas, "that Master Fundus there sometimes makes a noise during the night, especially just now, when he is getting his teeth, and I am obliged to creep out of my warm bed, although ever so tired, take him in my arms, walk about with him, and sing until my throat is sore, and my arms aching."

"Am I not right, then?" said Schubert.

"My back too is like to break," continued Kummas, "when I put the rogue on his feet, and let him totter up and down the room."

"And so does my wife complain," added Schubert. "Teaching them to walk must be a perfect martyrdom."

Kummas nodded assent, and went on,--"Neither am I any longer my own master. I cannot go where I will, or remain as long away as I please. The youngster is as a chain round my leg, which I must drag about. Besides, I must work hard, as my Christlieb needs many odds and ends, though the people in the village are very kind, and often send us presents. Afterwards will come the numerous diseases of children,--scarlet fever, measles, hooping-cough, &c., and then farewell to sleep; and all my earnings must go to the doctor and apothecary."

"That is precisely my case!" exclaimed Schubert in a loud tone.

"Softly! softly!" said Kummas, "or you will wake up my little rogue. Yes, I assure you, a whole night's playing on the violincello is a mere joke, compared with the watching all night by the bed of a sick child. I now see how much a mother has to do for her children, and how well founded are her claims to their gratitude."

"Therefore you are an old ass," said Schubert, quite angrily. "Shake yourself free of the child again."

"No!" answered Kummas firmly. "Some one must act the part of a mother to the poor thing, or it would perish, and that would be a sin. But after all, I must say, that my cares, my self-denial, and watchings are over-balanced by the pleasure I find in the child. When the little rascal smiles in my face, pinches my cheeks, or plays with my hair, all my trouble is forgotten. Nothing delights him so much as when I play a tune on the violin. Then is he all life; beats with his feet and claps his hands. He must be a musician, but a proper one. Not a miserable beer-fiddler, like you and me."

"I beg to decline the compliment," said the flute-player displeased. "You have become a fool about the child. I have only now to ask whether you are coming to play on Sunday along with us?"

"Since I know, from experience," replied Kummas, "how great is the trouble of bringing up a child, I cannot lend my aid by playing at dances, to destroy, perhaps, in one night the many years incessant labour of conscientious parents."

"What have we to do with that?" asked Schubert.

"Much, as I now perceive," replied the old man. "Yet I will not promise never to play again, were it only for the sake of Christlieb. But as long as I find some other kind of employment, and until the child is older, I will not."

"Do as you like, you old fool!" said Schubert in a passion, and went away.

Kummas comforted himself with the knowledge that he was doing right. "What! you young monkey; are you awake, and smiling? Oh! yes, I see you want your meat. So come away, and you shall have it directly."

CHAPTER IV.

THE BIRD-CATCHER.

"Take heed, boy, and pay great attention to my words!" said Kummas to his now ten-year-old Christlieb. "Look well at this thing which resembles a lady without legs or arms. See how its head is thrown back, with its round curls on each side, while its penetrating voice is even clearer than the voice of any dame. Now, what is the youngster laughing at? Eh! young sir?"

"It is only a violin, and not like a lady," said Christlieb laughing.

"Is the chick wiser than the hen? I tell you," said Kummas half scolding, "it is a lady; and violin, or violincello, is only its nickname. The throat of no lady, not even of a Catalina, can bring forth more beautiful and sustained notes than can the black throat of my violin. It is wonderful how the most insignificant of things may become, in the hands of a clever man, the source of inexhaustible treasures. Only think!--a few horse hairs rubbed against a few strings of cat-gut, placed across a piece of hollowed-out fir-wood, can be made to produce the most delicious tones! I tell you, boy, that a violin is a more productive mine than the famed one of Frieberg in the kingdom of Saxony. There a hundred miners do not dig out so much silver in a whole week as a single man, called Paganini, gets for one night's playing on the violin. But the lad looks at me as a cow does at a new gate! Well, well, you will understand this better by and by. Here, take hold of the violin with the left hand, and handle the bow so (showing the child how to use it). You must move the right hand regularly up and down, while the left hand, on the contrary, must spring nimbly like a squirrel from one place to another on the touch-board. If you wish to learn how to draw a good bow, place yourself in a corner, so that the wall may prevent your elbow from going out too far. The four strings are called G, D, A, E; but you will remember this rhyme perhaps better,---*Giess dir anis ein*!"

"Why not rather caraway-seed or peppermint?" asked a strange voice at the door. "Why must it be precisely anise, which, besides, is not good for the boy? Good-day, neighbour. I suppose you have never taken a glass of anything since you took home the foundling, and adopted him?"

Saying these words, the speaker came into the room. It was the aged Butter, the bird-catcher,--a good customer for the cages of Kummas.

"Good day, friend Butter," answered Kummas cheerfully. "What do we want more? We have now Butter in the house, and the bread must be forthcoming."

"The butter, I fear, will not taste well," replied the former; "it is too old. But tell me, is my bird-cage ready?"

"All except a few wires," said Kummas; "and I will send Christlieb with it immediately. Are you going to market already? Have you caught many birds to-day?"

"None worth speaking of; only a few larks and chaffinches. The larger birds come later;" and the old man drew out a lot of dead birds from under his cloak.

Christlieb quickly threw down the violin to look at the birds.

"Take care; they will bite you!" said Butter in a joke, shaking them in the face of the child.

"Poor things! how pretty they are with their beautiful feathers! But why are they all dead?" asked Christlieb in a tone of pity.

"Would you like to eat them alive?" said Butter.

"What!" exclaimed the boy in astonishment; "are they to be eaten?"

"Wherefore not, young friend?"

"The creatures are so very small, and when their feathers are off, they will be still less."

"That is quite true," replied Butter; "such a bird makes but two bites; and if one does not wish to leave the table as hungry as when he sat down, he must eat a dozen of them at least. Therefore rich people are rightly called bird-devourers."

"How much does one cost?" inquired Christlieb.

"For a halfpenny I will give you a lark or two finches."

"For a single halfpenny!" repeated the boy, much surprised. "Their feathers alone are worth more."

"I will make you a present of them," rejoined Butter, "if you will be at the trouble of plucking them off."

"Ah!" said Christlieb, "if they were alive, I would buy two chaffinches."

"I have a word to say to that," began Kummas; "where will you find meat for them?"

Christlieb made no answer; and Butter, changing the subject, said, "Neighbour, it is pretty cold in this room of yours; what will it be when the new year comes with its twenty degrees colder?"

"What!" exclaimed Kummas; "do you say it is cold here? It is an utter impossibility; for this morning I put into the stove sixteen dollars worth of wood!"

"Don't tell me such nonsense! who would believe that?"

"Well, then, look in and convince yourself," replied Kummas. "My violincello is burning there, and I can show you by writing that it cost me sixteen dollars."

"So, so, ah! I understand," continued Butter, laughing. "But what a dreadful spendthrift you are! No millionaire, no, not even a king, burns such precious wood."

"Therefore I can imagine myself somebody!" retorted Kummas, laughing heartily.

Christlieb, meanwhile, had been carefully examining the birds as they lay on the table. "I do not see," he said, turning round, "how they have been killed."

"That would not be easy to see," said Butter; "we are not on much ceremony with them, and just squeeze them to death in our hand. Look, I take my thumb and forefinger and press their little heart close to their wing. They open their beak, turn round their little eyes, and away they are."

At this description of how the poor things were put to death, the eyes of Christlieb filled with tears. With secret horror he looked at the unpitying, murderous fingers of the old man, whom his foster-father was accompanying to the door. He felt as if his cruel hand were pressing his own heart, and as if he could scarcely breathe. With a deep sigh, he said to his father when he came back, "And must the poor larks and chaffinches who sing so sweetly really be eaten?"

"Yes," answered Kummas; "and I do not think it altogether right. To eat singing birds is much the same as if I were to put violincellos and violins into the stove instead of common wood. The burning of the old piece of lumber, that was not worth any more mending, and in which you could no longer lie, was a mere exception. But truly, the greatest of all gluttons, the most voracious of all animals, is man. There is nothing safe from his palate. Earth, and air, and sea, the wilderness, and every corner of the world is ransacked for dainties to gratify it. However, I believe a simple meal is much better for health; one which willingly permits the feathered singers to pass their short lives unmolested."

When the bird-cage was finished, Christlieb was sent off with it to the cottage of the old man, which was situated a short way within a small wood. As the boy approached it, he found fresh cause for grief. He saw on many of the trees pieces of bent willow, to which were fastened loops of horse-hair; and here and there a poor little bird hanging in them, allured by the sight of the red berries close to where the nets were hung. He saw, at the same time, various other kinds of snares laid to entrap the unwary tenants of the grove.

For the first time, Christlieb entered the dwelling of the bird-catcher. He found it filled with cages, from which sounded all manner of chirping, piping, and singing. There was no one in the room except a little girl about his own age, who was busy playing on a small pipe the first part of an old march to four bulfinches.

Glad at having an excuse for giving up for a time her wearisome task, Malchen got up to receive the visitor, and take the cage from him. When Christlieb had softly delivered it into her hands, his whole attention was absorbed by the pretty prisoners, whose beautiful plumage he admired exceedingly; while Malchen answered all his questions with the utmost simplicity and childish pleasure.

In one cage there were chaffinches, in another larks, in others blackbirds, crossbills, lapwings, thrushes, and Bohemian chatterers and starlings. Christlieb was especially attracted by the sight of two greenfinches, who, by a singular contrivance, pulled up and down by their feet two small pails, in which was their food, holding them by a string attached to the cage for that purpose, until they were satisfied. This sight was, however, by no means pleasing to Christlieb; it rather made him sad, when he saw how often the pail slipped away before the poor little bird could get either one grain of seed, or one drop of water.

"How are they taught to do this?" asked Christlieb, surprised at the seemingly rational act of the tiny creatures.

"By hunger and thirst," replied Malchen. "Before they can be brought to pull up their seed and water, they are almost dying of hunger."

"Do they likewise sing?" he again asked.

"Not much," answered the girl; "only a few notes. But do you know that birds and animals have a language of their own?" And she began to tell the wondering boy a great many things which she had heard her grandfather repeat.

"I should like to be able to know also what they say," answered Christlieb.

"You must just pay great attention," said the little Malchen, "and you can learn it yourself."

"Are all birds here to be killed?" asked Christlieb.

"No; not these ones," replied Malchen. "They are sold alive. Only we cannot keep them long, for then their meat costs more than they are worth."

"I should like very much to have a goldfinch," said Christlieb, "or a thrush."

"Oh, no!" cried the little girl; "a starling would be much nicer; it is such a droll bird, and can learn to speak like a man."

"Is that true?" asked Christlieb doubtingly.

"Quite true; only his tongue must be loosened," replied Malchen.

Christlieb determined to try and get as much money as would buy a speaking bird; and in this hope he took great pains to learn to play on the violin, in the expectation of learning something.

How joyfully he ran home one day, when a traveller had given him twopence for playing a tune, and accompanying it with his clear sweet voice. This was the beginning of a treasure, which every week he divided most faithfully with his dear foster-father.

CHAPTER V.

THE SINGULAR MEETING.

Two years had now passed away, and harvest, with its rejoicings and feasts, was at hand. The evening preceding one of the festivals, our Fundus, now twelve years of age, was standing before a rather roughly constructed music-stand, on which was placed a sheet of written notes for the violin. He was again rehearsing what, on the succeeding day, he had to perform, and played and sung his appointed parts alternately. Kummas, whose hair had now become white, sat listening in his arm-chair, congratulating himself on having made such a fine player of the child. He nodded time with his head, and his eyes sparkled with delight, as the youthful scholar succeeded in mastering a difficult passage far beyond the expectation of the old musician. The very starling, who had been long asleep in its accustomed place (the back of the old man's chair), awoke and became quite merry, screaming an accompaniment to its young master.

At length the rehearsal was ended, and Christlieb packed up his music, awaiting the judgment of his preceptor.

The old man, hiding his delight, said, "Well, I hope you will get on to-morrow, only be sure and keep the time. Remember there is a great difference playing before four eyes, and playing in the church before four hundred. However, don't let this remark make you afraid."

Kummas had not received much education; but he was of opinion that a child might be spoiled through too much praise, and therefore he was very sparing in his commendation. However, when Christlieb was fast asleep, he gave vent to his joy while, as usual, smoking his pipe before he went to bed. With a grateful heart he thanked God that in the foundling there was given to him a support and a pleasure for his old age. All his privations and cares were richly repaid by the admirable behaviour of the boy, with whom he would not part for any worldly consideration whatever.

The church festival, with music, singing, prayers, and sermon, was now over, and the churchyard filled with people returning to their various homes. In the midst of them were the pastor and the schoolmaster, with the happy Kummas at their side; while Christlieb, with his violin under his arm, followed at a respectful distance.

"That foster-son of yours is a fine youth," began the pastor.

"He is like a pearl in a dirty oyster-shell," responded the schoolmaster.

"Your simile is rather a lame one," said the priest; "for neither is our village nor the house of Kummas like a dirty oyster-shell, as the owner of the latter has now become an honest Christian; yet it is true that Christlieb is not in his proper place here. He should be sent where he can have more advantage than with us."

"He far excels all my pupils," continued the teacher; "and even in Latin he is well advanced. He ought to study."

"Aye, aye," said Kummas, smiling with pleasure; "but to study, I am told, costs a deal of money, and I have none. If I could do as I wished, I would like to make the boy a fine musician,--one who would bring my art to honour. I had an idea of sending him to some band-master in a town, in order that he might have more teaching; yet it will be very hard for me to part with him, as he now plays more than I do, and brings more bread into the house. To be sure that would be made up for were he to become a little Paganini."

"Certainly," said the pastor, laughing. "We shall see what time will do. Meanwhile, take care that Christlieb remains as modest and gentle as he is now; as that makes him well-pleasing in the sight of God, as well as of men."

When the pastor and the schoolmaster had left, Kummas went and spoke to Butter, whom he saw standing near him.

"Your Fundus played and sang to-day like a lark. My Malchen was all ear and eye. There they go like brother and sister. But tell me, what does the boy do with all the birds he buys from me? I thought by this time that your room would be quite full of them; but I only see the starling marching about at its ease. Besides, he has a shocking taste; for he buys almost only those which are good for nothing, except to twist off their heads, and lay them in the frying-pan."

"Indeed! I know nothing about the matter," answered Kummas, "and never ask him; for, as I am sure he does not waste the little money he gets, I let him do whatever he likes with his few halfpence."

"I suppose you think, at the same time, I have no cause to complain of his spending his money in this way?" Saying these words, the old men separated.

On the same Sunday, Christlieb, accompanied by Malchen, came out of the bird-catcher's house. "Stop a minute," said he to the young girl, taking out of her hand a finch, round whose right leg he fastened a small piece of red thread, but not very tightly.

"Why do you do that?" asked Malchen.

"Oh! it is a fancy of mine," said Christlieb, taking hold of the bird, and bidding the girl good-bye; who looked after him with curiosity before she again went into the house.

Christlieb went a considerable way into the wood. "Don't be afraid," he said softly to the little bird, whose heart he felt beating as he held the terrified creature in his hand; "from me you have nothing to fear. Perhaps your young ones are dying with hunger, for want of you, in their solitary nest; or your father and mother are seeking you everywhere, calling to you to come back to them. Now take care, little stupid thing, and don't let wicked boys catch you by mock whistles, mock pipes, or mock food; and there, now, fly away!" With these words he opened his hand, and the finch, not needing to be told twice, flew quickly away. Christlieb looked after it until it disappeared in the blue distance. He then took a piece of paper out of his pocket, on which he made a small mark with a pencil. "Twenty-six finches," he repeated to himself, "nineteen larks, five thrushes, nine lapwings, two goldfinches, three blackbirds,--four-and-sixty birds I have saved from death or imprisonment.--Hurrah! hurrah!"

The same evening, Christlieb was again playing; and in the same room of that inn in which his foster-father had played twelve years before,--at the door of which he had found him. Waltzes, country dances, galops, quadrilles, and all manner of tunes dropped from his hand like water. He played unweariedly, although sleep every now and then shut his eyes, and the player of the violincello had to give him a gentle push with the point of his bow at the end of the hundredth-time-played pieces. Meanwhile, Kummas enjoyed rest at home. The grateful foundling now supplied his place, which he felt it neither difficult nor unpleasant to do. Obedient to the command of his father, he steadfastly refused to taste either beer or brandy, and contented himself with pure water,--an abstinence not at all disagreeable to the other musicians, as by that means their portions were the larger. About three o'clock in the morning, the dance ended, and dancers and musicians left the inn; all except Christlieb, who laid himself down on a bench, near the stove in the lower room, and slept for three hours the pleasant sleep of youth and weariedness. When he awoke, the landlady gave him a cup of delicious coffee, and a piece of fine cake, after partaking which he prepared for his walk home.

With his violin under his arm, and twelve groschens in his pocket, Christlieb descended the steps which led from the inn door to the road. His eye fell upon the manger, which always stood ready for horses passing with travellers. He looked at it much affected, as he thought, Who knows but that may be the very one in which I was found twelve years since! What would have become of me had not Kummas taken me with him? Feelings of gratitude to his foster-father filled his heart. Ah! why had his parents deserted him? How had the poor infant offended them, thus to be driven from them? How often have I watched the care which geese, hens, dogs, cats, little birds, and all animals take care of their young ones,--defending them at the risk of their own lives! Even the defenceless insect, the ant, when a ruthless hand destroys its nest, first tries to save its eggs,--and yet, has a heartless mother forsaken me? Or may I not have been taken from her by force, or stealth?---in which case she will be more unhappy than I am. But the sadness of youth resembles a soap-bubble, which, when broken, leaves no trace behind; and with the rising of the golden sun, Christlieb's sorrow vanished. Although it was November, the weather was fine, and there still were some vestiges of verdure to be seen. With a merry heart, and a quiet conscience, Christlieb pursued his journey homewards, while he gave outward expression to his gladness by playing a beautiful church melody on his violin.

An echo in the neighbouring wood gave back the clear notes, accompanied by those of all the birds who had not fled with summer. This singing allured him to his favourite spot, where the rustling of the leaves of the trees greeted him like the voices of old acquaintances. He slung his instrument over his shoulder, and, like a squirrel, sprung up a tall pine tree, where, among its green branches, he comfortably seated himself. From this leafy height there was soon heard the cheerful note of the cuckoo, the melancholy song of the yellow thrush, the melting call of the nightingale, the monotonous cry of the crow; in short, all the feathered tribe seemed to have met in this one spot, in order to let each other hear their different music. And Christlieb, the sole artist and imitator of the various notes, rejoiced beyond measure, when the whole flock of the still remaining birds, allured by the sounds, came and flew around him. Still more zealously did he copy on his obedient violin the language of the feathered tribe, when the whole concert was destroyed and quickly ended, by the rattling of carriage wheels. In a moment, Christlieb was down the tree, and, led by curiosity to take a peep at the supposed travellers, he speedily made up to the carriage. It was a handsome equipage, whose driver no sooner saw Christlieb, than he called out, seemingly very ill pleased, "What are you about, young sir? Does the young gentleman think I have nothing else to do but keep my mouth open, shouting after him, instead of swallowing the good soup of the postmaster? Come, make haste and get in!" Saying these words, the man leapt from the driving box, and opened the door of the carriage. "And now," continued he, muttering to himself in a bad humour, "we have to wait for the tutor, who, full of anxiety, is seeking up and down for his idle pupil."

When the driver, after letting down the steps, looked round for the object of his wrath, the astonished Christlieb was no longer to be seen, which gave rise to a fresh burst of angry words and oaths. The puzzled violin player had run away as fast as he could, and was now again within the wood, when his flying steps were arrested by another person, who came up to him, looking very exhausted and tired, and likewise very angry. "Balduin! Balduin!" he exclaimed, in a tone of vexation and displeasure, "will this thoughtlessness never end, which annoys and torments every one connected with you? Where have you been? Since you left the carriage under a pretext of only remaining away a few minutes, you have remained almost an hour! But how is this?" he continued in surprise. "Where have you exchanged your dress? and how did you get this instrument?"

The stranger stretched out his hand to take hold of the violin, whose possessor, however, firmly retained it, and took to his heels, flying through the wood as if winged.

He still, at a considerable distance, heard the voice of his pursuer entreating him to remain.

He arrived at home out of breath, and had scarcely time to put away his violin, when the bell rang for school; so that for some hours, he had to keep his adventure to himself.

"Only think, father!"--With these words, he entered the small room, in which, besides Kummas, he found the old bird-catcher, who looked at him with an angry countenance, and his father, too, seemed unusually disconcerted.

"There comes the young good-for-nothing," said Butter. "Bird-thief, and not Christlieb, should he be called."

Christlieb's words stuck in his throat at this salutation; and, much amazed and perplexed, he looked at the old man, to see whether he were speaking in jest or in earnest. But his father ended his doubt by saying, in a serious tone of voice, "What have you done, Christlieb? Confess the truth."

A deep red suffused Christlieb's face, as, with the greatest faithfulness, he related what had happened to him.

When he had finished, Butter said with bitterness, "So you wish to make us believe that a runaway boy, who had escaped from his tutor, played the trick, and not you, you young rascal, but your ghost (*doppelgänger*)! A likely story, forsooth! Will you still deny that you broke and destroyed all my nets?--that you let twelve thrushes, eighteen finches, nine-and-twenty other birds, not to speak of the very small ones, escape? Such a number I never caught at once in my life; and while I ran full of joy into the house, to get my old wife and Malchen to come and help me, the rascal falls upon the whole, tears my snares to pieces, sets all the birds at liberty, and then laughs at me scornfully from behind a bush, when I try to catch him."

"I never did such a thing," maintained Christlieb, shocked.

"What!" cried Butter, in a greater passion than ever; "will you give me the lie to my face? Have I become so blind that I no longer know you when I see you? Besides, was not Malchen, who thinks so much of you, there as a witness? And do we not know, likewise, that, in your folly, you wish there was not a bird-catcher in all the world, and that all the birds were free?"

"Acknowledge your fault, my son," said Kummas mildly, "and we may be able to make all right again."

"But I have not done what Butter says," answered Christlieb, weeping.

"Friend," said Kummas, "I really know not what to think of all this. It is true that Christlieb has never once deceived me, and----"

"You are an old blockhead, with your Christlieb!" passionately broke out Butter, interrupting him. "It will be worse for him in the end; for, as you give me no satisfaction, I am determined to have him punished; and, as sure as my name is Butter, the boy shall have a few days in the dungeon."

CHAPTER VI.

THE UNDESERVED PUNISHMENT.

The bird-catcher put his threat into execution, and our Christlieb was really taken to the dungeon in the prison. The poor boy had been a long day, and a still longer night, in the damp dismal place, when, early on the second morning, he heard a well-known voice calling to him through the bars of the narrow window. Christlieb left his miserable straw pallet, and quickly approaching the window, said in a cheerful voice, "Is that you, father?"

"How are you, my boy?" asked Kummas in a pitying tone. "I fear bread and water will not taste well here?"

"Oh! that is the least of it," answered Christlieb. "I would not mind that, were it not so dismally cold; and I weary, having nothing to do."

"Have you nothing else to plague you?--No evil conscience?" said the old man, somewhat sadly.

The boy burst into a flood of tears, and said, amidst sobs, "Father, do not make me more unhappy in my trouble! Indeed, I am not guilty."

"I believe you, my son," said Kummas with a lighter heart, "although appearances are certainly very much against you. But if we are innocent, we may be happy even in a dungeon. Think of the good Joseph, who was in prison for many years, while you are to be only three days in this black hole."

"That is nothing, father; but I cannot bear to think of the shame, and of being pointed at by all the villagers.

"Let them point at you as they like," said Kummas, comforting him; "so long as you are not guilty, it does not matter. And who knows why God has sent you this cross? For a wise purpose, be assured. Look here! I have brought you a drop of warm beer, if I only knew how to get it down to you without spilling it." He fastened a piece of string to the small can, and the vessel, with its smoking contents, reached Christlieb in safety.

"Does it taste well?" asked Kummas when he saw its arrival safely below. "I cooked it myself."

"Yes!" answered Christlieb, thanking him; "but you have put in such a quantity of pepper, that it has almost burnt my throat."

"Aye!" replied the pleased warm-beer-brewer, "I did that purposely, to keep out the cold. Now, would you like anything else?"

"I should like to play on the violin," said Christlieb eagerly.

"Perhaps that would not be permitted," answered Kummas, "even if we could get the violin through the bars. The jailor might be angry if he heard a noise in the prison, so you would need to play quite pianissimo. We shall see about it; and in the meantime, good bye."

"Do not forget to feed the starling," cried Christlieb, as Kummas went away.

Scarcely was the old man gone, when Christlieb, who had lain down again in his corner, heard some one else call out softly, "Christlieb, Christlieb! Hear me, and don't be angry at me."

"I will not speak to you," said Christlieb. "You are a serpent!"

"Ah! dear Christlieb, do hear me!" said Malchen, for it was she who had come to comfort her playmate. But Christlieb would not move from his place in the corner of the dingy prison.

"Christlieb!" continued the young girl, weeping, "can you deny that I saw you when you pulled the nets in pieces?"

"I tell you I will not speak to you," reiterated Christlieb in an angry tone.

"Could I help confessing the truth to my grandfather when he called me as a witness? I have not slept all night thinking of you, and have ran here at the risk of being scolded. Forgive me, Christlieb, for having seen you destroy the nets the day before yesterday, and for being the means of bringing you into this place."

"So you still maintain that you really saw me, and that I was the person who did the mischief! Have I not always bought the birds, and honestly paid for them? Have I ever all my life let even a sparrow escape from you?"

Malchen could not make any answer to this reproach; but only entreated the more earnestly to be forgiven, saying, "Do let us be friends again, Christlieb!"

"Whenever I come out of this place," answered Christlieb proudly, "I will go far away from you all, to Turin, or to some other distant town; and there become a Paganini, and earn eight hundred dollars every night by playing on my violin; then, when I am rich, I will come back with a carriage and four horses, and take my foster-father, who believes that I did not destroy the nets, away with me. But you and your grandfather, I will neither look at nor speak to."

"You will do no such thing," answered Malchen confidently.

"But I will!" maintained Christlieb resolutely.

"No, no!" answered his little companion; "I know you better than to believe it. And now, since you have spoken to me, I am sure you are no longer angry with me."

"You are mistaken," said Christlieb; but in rather a smoother voice.

"Shall I come again to see you here?" asked Malchen.

Christlieb made no reply; and the kind-hearted little maiden again asked the question.

"Shall I come back again? If you do not answer me when I have counted three, then I will remain away. Once, twice, thrice. Shall I, or shall I not come?"

"Yes, you may come," cried Christlieb, as he saw Malchen leaving the window. A piece of paper with something wrapped in it, was thrown down to him, which he quickly opened, and found a nice little cake, brought by Malchen, who was now out of sight. This mark of sympathy cheered him; and his imprisonment became less unbearable.

The accident which had brought him into disgrace was not without weighty consequences. Butter was irreconcileable, and prohibited his little granddaughter from speaking to our hero. The children of the village teased him, and the elder persons looked at him with suspicion. These circumstances induced Kummas to try and find some other quarters for his foster-son, as soon as the latter was confirmed. In this the old musician succeeded, by means of a friend in a neighbouring small town, from whom Christlieb had received some lessons. This person procured for him the situation of a pupil with the principal bandmaster of a large town at a considerable distance from the village where he now was.

"Trust in God, do what is right, and fear no man," said Kummas to his weeping Christlieb, as, laden like a camel, the poor boy stood ready for his journey; "'and then the sky will be full of music,' as we are accustomed to say. You must become a clever fellow. I do not say this for your sake alone, but also for my own; as I must, in your absence, live very sparingly; but this I will gladly do, believing that a time of plenty will follow, which I hope through you to see. Remember, that as long as God gives you sound limbs, it is in your own power to keep sorrow from yourself, cares from me, and to drive away wrinkles from my brow; therefore, beat the drum, sound the trumpet, blow the horn, and play on the violin, with all your heart; for music is a lady, and, you know, all ladies wish to be admired. Should death, with his bony hand and ruthless scythe mow me down before you come back as a master in your art, then the villagers, as they walk over my grave, will not scornfully say, 'Here lies a poor fiddler;' but they will add, 'he, at least, did one good action when he----'" Here the old man stopped, not able, from emotion, to proceed; and, ashamed of his tears, he hid his face on Christlieb's shoulder, upon whose head the pet starling had perched itself.

Lifting down the bird, Christlieb said, "Perhaps you would not like to keep the bird, father?"

"No, my son," answered the latter; "I might, perhaps, forget to feed it, and it might die of hunger, or of thirst."

"Then farewell, father." They embraced each other, and Christlieb went away. Shunning the houses of the villagers, of whom he had already taken leave, Christlieb took the road to the wood. When he reached his favourite spot, taking the starling from his shoulder, he said to it, "Go now, my little bird, to your companions among the trees!" He threw it up into the air; but after a short flight it came back, and again alighted on the shoulder of its master. "What! wilt thou not go?" he said, much affected. "Poor bird, I cannot keep thee." He threw it again from him, and again the little creature came back. Upon this he went straight to the house of the bird-catcher, and luckily saw Malchen standing at the door cleaning some utensils. She became pale at the sight of Christlieb, and said quickly, "What do you want here? My grandfather is sitting at the window."

"Malchen," said Christlieb hastily, "you must do me a favour. Here is my starling, who will not leave me. You must keep it, or afterwards set it at liberty."

The young girl took the bird, and went into the house with it. Christlieb went close to the window where the old man sat reading.

"Father Butter," he began firmly, "you have ordered me never to come within your door. Give me your hand, then, out at the window, and say, at parting, that you will not any longer be angry with me."

Butter looked up, and shook his head at the boy.

"Father!" repeated Christlieb entreatingly, "you have let many suns set on your wrath; give me your hand."

"If you will confess your fault," said the old man, relenting a little.

"Let us say no more about that," answered Christlieb. "I may or I may not have done it. You know we are all sinners."

At length the bird-catcher yielded, put his hand out at the window, and said, "I forgive you! Go in peace."

"A thousand thanks, father," answered Christlieb, well pleased. "Farewell!" and he was speedily out of sight; while Malchen, with tears in her eyes, looked after her playmate.

CHAPTER VII.

THE TOWN MUSICIAN.

After six days' walking, Christlieb reached the place of his destination. The town musician (*stadt-musikus*), as is the case in many places, had his dwelling in the tower of the Cathedral, which was glittering under the rays of the setting sun as Christlieb turned his steps towards the direction in which it lay. In order to gain strength to ascend its long winding stair, he seated himself on a stone bench, which he saw before one of the houses in the market-place, and here waited to cool himself before he ventured to take a draught of the sparkling water, which was emptying itself in silver streams from many jets into the basin of the large fountain which stood in the centre of the square. Like a bunch of roots which a boy dipped into it, Christlieb would have liked a bath too in the pure element. "So this is the evening of a feast day!" cried the boy to a companion, who was passing near the fountain; "look, there is the trumpeter with his brass thing at his mouth."

Christlieb also looked up to where the boy was pointing, and on the railed gallery which ran round a part of the tower, he saw the performer with his brazen trumpet glancing in the bright golden sunlight, from which, in sublime full tones, was poured forth the beautiful church melody, beginning, "Who lets the Lord direct his way."

In a more cheering manner the town musician could not have greeted his new pupil, nor in a way which went more to the heart of the solitary child. Full of confidence, and rid of the anxiety which it was natural at such a time to feel, Christlieb approached the tower.

When he had reached it and knocked, a maid-servant made her appearance, whose countenance was not very pleasant looking. "What do you want?" she asked in a sharp voice.

"I wish to see the town musician," said Christlieb diffidently.

"Mr. Dilling," she cried to a person within, "here is a country boy who wants to see you."

Mr. Dilling, a thin little man of about fifty, appeared, took the letter of recommendation out of Christlieb's hand, read it hastily, and told the boy to put down his bundle. The wife of the master musician, a portly dame, then took him in, and acquainted him with the various duties he would have to perform, which Christlieb thought equal to those of a second servant. As it was supposed the youth would be tired after his long journey, he was given something to eat, and the servant showed him where he was to sleep. His bed was in a corner of the church tower, and was no worse than the one he had left at home. Being very wearied, he soon fell into a sound sleep. After the lapse of a few hours, he was awakened by a dull whirring sort of sound, followed by the ringing of a bell, which seemed to be right above his head. He looked up, and saw five or six figures ascending a wooden stair, which was close to his bed. These were doubtless his new companions; and as they returned, one of them said to the others, "There lies my successor; I have long enough been the drudge! Now that country clown may see how he likes it."

The person who was carrying the light turned quickly round, and said to the other who had spoken, "What! are you better than the rest, I wonder? Hold that idle tongue of yours, else I will shut your mouth in a way you don't like."

All again was quiet, except the regular movement of the pendulum of the church clock, which kept Christlieb awake for a short time longer.

Before five o'clock had struck, the shrill voice of the maid called to him to get up and go to the baker's for the bread for breakfast.

"I will likewise," she added, "lower down the cask for the water in the basket, and before you come up again you must fill it with fresh water from the fountain."

Christlieb quickly dressed himself to obey his orders, and with the money in his hand to pay for the bread, he groped his way down the dark narrow winding stair. When he came back from the baker's, he saw coming down in a basket, by means of a strong rope, the cask for the water. This mode of descending and ascending pleased him very much; and if he had dared, he would liked to have been pulled up himself in this way. When the watchful maid saw that all was right, she again drew up the basket with its contents. Before Christlieb followed, he enjoyed the luxury of bathing his face and breast in the sparkling water of the fountain, which refreshed him exceedingly. There awaited him a formidable battery of boots and shoes to clean, which new sort of work cost him no small exertion. Before he began he got a cup of coffee, and ate a roll while brushing and polishing. During his absence his companions must have risen; for he heard the voice of his master saying, "Rupel, blow the morning greeting, and take the melody, 'Awake, awake, the voice of morning calls.' This will do for the sluggards in the town."

The young man thus addressed came out with the trumpet in his hand. Christlieb politely wished him "Good morning," which the other courteously answered, and stepped out on to the small gallery, scarcely two paces distant from the busy shoe-black. The trumpet now began to sound in the deep bass, then ascended to a second and a third, rested for a time at the fifth, repeating the melody to the sleeping inhabitants beneath. At the second strophe, it seemed to Christlieb as if an angel were calling the world to judgment, so sublime and powerful were the sounds brought forth by the skilful player. The very tower seemed to shake; and Christlieb, enraptured, folded his hands across his breast, while his eyes filled with tears. The returning artiste saw the effect which his playing produced, and felt flattered, in no small degree, by the mute praise of the peasant boy.

The sublime hymn was followed by an ear-splitting concert in the room of the *stadt-musikus*.

"Beautiful Minka, I must leave thee," lamented, in sorrowful tones, the clarionet.

"Let us be merry all," played briskly the cheerful violin, with many beautiful variations.

"I am not lonely nor alone," breathed forth the flute in a delicious fantasia.

"I fear not death," muttered the basson.

The oboe, in an imperfect croaking tone, exercised itself in a difficult passage, which it repeated a hundred times over, resembling a ladder which wanted some of its steps.

Of all the instruments the bugle had the preference, which was now tortured by one of the youngest pupils. Certainly had Bishop Hatto fallen on this method of frightening away the rats, he would not have found it necessary to build the well-known tower in the middle of the Rhine. Whoever is no friend to rat powder, or table flattery, has only to get such a player into his house, in order to free himself from all sorts of vermin. Even the crows, who are not peculiarly fastidious in their musical taste, fled affrighted from the top of the steeple,--their chosen resting-place.

Into this assembly Christlieb was ushered when he had finished his work. At his entrance, the grumbling, muttering, lively, and sad tones ceased, while the youthful players all looked, with eyes wide open, at the new comer. Mr. Dilling placed Christlieb before a music-stand, put a violin and a bow into his hands, and desired to hear a proof of his skill, choosing for that purpose one of Pleyel's sonatas. Christlieb obeyed; but played very badly. The boys laughed maliciously; the master frowned; and only Rupel, the assistant, said at once, "Mr. Dilling, how can you expect the boy to play when his hands are still shaking from the effects of brushing the boots and shoes?"

The master acknowledged he was right, and therefore sent Christlieb away to rest himself; who gladly went out on the gallery to look around him. How beautiful was the view from this place! The houses, with their smoking chimneys, the streets, with their busy passengers, all lay at his feet. Beyond were the blue mountains, with a river winding itself at their base; and behind them arose the bright morning sun; while beautiful gardens, with trees, flowers, and shrubs, were scattered around the town in every direction. An hour flew away, Christlieb knew not how.

"Are your hands steady now?" called out his master to him from the window. Christlieb went in, and this trial was more successful than his former one had been. The master nodded his satisfaction; the pupils stared; and Rupel said to them, "You see the country clown plays you all to sticks; therefore you must show him respect."

"Can you play on any other instrument except the violin?" asked Mr. Dilling.

"I can play a little on the violincello," answered Christlieb.

"That is nothing," continued the master; "a *stadt-musikus* must have every instrument in his power, although he may excel in one more than the rest."

Under the guidance of Mr. Dilling, the whole of the pupils were now to play an overture; and to each was duly assigned his part. Besides the favourite and current names which the fiery gentleman bestowed on his pupils, such as ox, ass, blockhead, dunse, &c., he likewise dealt out to them sundry knocks on the head and pinches of the ears; and as for the unfortunate player of the bugle, the time was taught him by blows on his back. Christlieb was very much terrified, but escaped this time with the mere fright. The same day he learnt the triangle, the cymbals, and how to beat the large drum, as well as to make a trial with the kettle-drums. This instruction was given him by Rupel the assistant, who had entirely won the affection of Christlieb, and who was indeed liked much better by all the pupils than the master himself.

The dinner, with which the others in secret all found fault, tasted extremely good to Christlieb, who had never eaten anything so nice. When, with twilight, the lessons and exercises were ended, the master and his assistant went into the town to amuse themselves, while the scholars were left behind to copy music and rule paper. There devolved on Christlieb, as the last comer, the duty of attending to the clock, and of ringing the evening bells. After all this was done, he had still time to eat, to dress, and to sleep.

CHAPTER VIII.

THE CORRESPONDENCE.

Summer had nearly passed away, when the solitary Kummas received, quite unexpectedly, a letter from his foster-son. It was the first, and therefore a source of great joy to the old man. The letter began as follows:--

"DEAR FATHER,--It will please me very much to know that you are quite well. I am thankful to say, that since I left you, I have been in perfect health, and I have grown much taller, which is shown by the sleeves of my jacket, as they are now almost up to my elbows. I would not even yet have been able to write to you (as I had no money to pay the postage, and did not wish to put you to the expense of it) had not a stranger, who was up the *tower* to see the fine view, offered to take my letter free. I live here very comfortably; and when I ring the evening bells, I always turn my eyes in your direction. I often wish I had wings to fly to you, and give you a surprise. I have plenty to do; you know already that I have to ring the bells every night; but besides this, when there is a funeral of any distinguished person, or when it is a feast-day, we have to ring all the bells; and that takes the whole of us to do. You see, dear father, it is a kind of music, and therefore the business of the town musician. Then I have all the boots and shoes to clean; to carry the bread from the baker's, and the water from the well; all the instruments to look after, and the church clock to keep right, and, on market days, I carry home the basket of provisions, walking behind my mistress, and run messages to the town when anything is wanted. When I am very heavily laden, I pack all into the basket, and Hannel the cook draws them up in it. Indeed, we sometimes draw up each other, which is good fun. However, I had a trick played on me lately, which was not very pleasant. We had been at a concert until late in the night, and my companions were this time obliged to help to carry home the instruments. Contrary to custom, they were very kind to me; packed the instruments carefully in the basket, and urged me to go likewise into it, faithfully promising to draw me up as soon as they reached the landing-place. They drew me up quickly enough until I was about half way; then the basket stood still, and I could not move it in the least. A loud laugh from the gallery soon informed me what the rogues had done. Only think, father, of my swinging up there in the middle of the night! and there they meant me to swing until morning. My seat was a very bad one; for I now found that they had so placed the instruments that I could not move. I sat on the sharp edges of the violin-cases, while the kettledrums lay on my stretched-out legs, and the mouths of the bugles and horns pierced into my sides. I could scarcely keep my eyes open, I was so sleepy; and, to make matters worse, it began to rain. I then became frightened lest the instruments should get injured, and cried out for help; but no answer came. It was all dark and silent above me. In my despair, I seized the drum-sticks, and began at first to play gently; but as this was of no avail, I thundered out on them in C, and then in G. This worked like a charm; and, continuing to rattle on the drum, I was drawn up as quick as lightning, when my comrades began to abuse me for the dreadful noise I was making. I, however, was not to blame, and threatened to tell the master what they had done; so, in the end, they were glad to get me, by smooth speeches, to say nothing.

"But they played me many wicked tricks; sometimes calling out 'Fire! fire!' and awakening me to give the alarm from the tower-bell to the people in the town; sometimes putting dead mice in my bed. But the worst thing they did was at a concert about a week ago, where I was to play on the violin, when they rubbed the bow over with grease. The master had expected to receive great applause by my playing; and you may fancy his and my consternation, when not a single note could I bring forth. For this piece of mischief, however, they were soundly thrashed; and now, I think they will leave me in peace. How much I wish you could hear the beautiful variations I have learnt, which the great Rhode of Paris composed. They are as beautiful as the voice of Malchen when she sings. What does Malchen do now, father? Is she still with her grandfather? and is my starling yet alive? Remember me to her, as well as to old Butter, the pastor, and the schoolmaster. My master's best violin cost forty dollars; and, would you believe it! there are violins which cost four and six hundred dollars! A single small violin of wood to cost as much as three or four small houses in our village! I can play on eight different instruments; but I detest the oboe, with its croaking voice. My master is very passionate; but I do not get so many cuffs as the others, although they always push me into the breach when they have done anything wrong. The mistress likes very much to scold; therefore I go out of her way as much as possible. The assistant Rupel is very kind to me; and when we are alone, we play beautiful duets together. Dear father, I would like to send you a little present, or some money; but I have not one farthing, although I spend nothing, and write music half the night. Perhaps afterwards I shall become only the richer for being now so poor. But I must finish, for my lamp is almost out, and my eyes will scarcely keep open. So excuse all the blots, and believe me, your affectionate and dutiful son,

"CHRISTLIEB FUNDUS."

About a fortnight after this letter had been despatched, a loud rapping was heard at the door at the foot of the tower. Christlieb looked out, and saw a countryman standing, who had a small basket in his hand, and who beckoned to Christlieb to come and speak to him. The latter immediately ran down.

"Are you Master Christlieb Fundus from Gelenau, the pupil of the town musician?" asked the man.

"Yes!" answered Christlieb; upon which the man handed him a letter, and the small basket, saying, "I have many greetings to you,--you will know from whom,--from old Butter and his little granddaughter; and from the old man the fiddler of Gelenau. If the berries in the basket are all gone to juice, it's not my fault; you will only be saved the trouble of eating them." The countryman laughed; and after receiving Christlieb's thanks, went away. Christlieb hastily opened the letter, which was from Malchen, and read:--

"DEAR CHRISTLIEB,--Your long, long letter we have all read; and it made us very happy to hear of your welfare. I have nothing to entertain you with in return; for there is no news here, everything goes on in the old jog-trot fashion. But how learned you have become! I could not understand parts of your letter, until father Kummas explained them. I knew not what an oboe was, nor anything of Rhode, or of his variations. If I were you, I would have the idle fellows who are so mischievous put into the dungeon, until they learnt to behave better. The schoolmaster has got a new velvet cap, and the church clock a new pointer. Your starling is still alive, and almost eats me up,--that is, my few half-pence. But for your sake I keep it, although my grandfather is always scolding about it.

"With this you will receive a small basket, containing some bramble and whortleberries, of which you used to be so fond. When you become a Paganini, and can get, as Kummas says, ever so many dollars for one night's playing, then send me a stylish cap back in the basket, or something very fine from the town. Above all things, don't become proud, or I shall vex myself to death. Don't let your companions see the basket for fear they steal the berries from you; and be sure and wash the blue stains from your lips, so that they may know nothing about them. Now, good-bye, says your friend,

"MALCHEN."

Christlieb put his letter in the most private corner of his abode, and ate the fruit as soon as possible,--though he had to use a spoon for the purpose, as in consequence of their long carriage they were sadly bruised. As to the wish of the kind giver for a stylish cap from the town, that, alas! he would be unable to send, until he indeed became a Paganini.

CHAPTER IX.

THE JOURNEY ON THE ICE.

The winter with its frost and snow had passed away, the cold of which had been severely felt by the dwellers in the house of the town musician, as from its high and exposed situation no storm passed without their experiencing its chilling effects. Christlieb had the prospect of soon being relieved from his duties as youngest, for a new pupil was expected at Easter. He was much pleased at this, as he hoped then to be able to earn a few pence, which now was entirely out of his power, never having one moment at his own disposal.

During the carnival there was a grand entertainment at a much-frequented place of amusement, a few miles distant from the town, and lying on the opposite side of the river. As usual, Christlieb was the last to leave, and, laden with the kettle-drums, was following his companions home, who, having less to carry, were already across the river before Christlieb had reached it. The stream was still covered with strong ice, although it had been thawing for several days, and the water was standing some inches above the ice. The air was very warm, indeed almost sultry. The water bubbled up as if boiling wherever an opening in the frozen surface was seen, and every now and then a loud cracking of the ice was heard. At a distance guns were fired to announce its breaking up to the inhabitants on the banks of the river. Christlieb saw, heard, and trembled; he hesitated for an instant before venturing on the ice, but, soon regaining courage, boldly stept on it. His comrades had just gone over before him; there was no bridge near, nor any means of getting to the other side; he saw the twinkling small light in the tower inviting him to proceed! With one drum on his back, and the other hanging before his breast, he had gained his way half across in safety, when suddenly the treacherous ice gave way just a few steps from him. It broke, raised itself up, and then yielding to the flood of water, moved on, and finally sank beneath the overwhelming power of the watery element, which spread itself again over the glassy surface. Christlieb stood petrified, then with trembling limbs ran to look for some safer place where he might be able still to get to the opposite bank. Wherever he looked, he saw the same comfortless prospect. He now tried to return to the side he had left; but he had scarcely proceeded twenty steps, when the whole body of ice broke from the banks, and he was slowly borne away with it. In the houses of the town which lay nearest to the rising waters lights were glancing backwards and forwards, and on every side was heard the cry, "The ice is breaking up!"

"He had fallen upon his knees on the ice."

Christlieb also shouted, in the hope of finding help; but no answer came. All the bells were set a-ringing, whose tones, mingling with the crashing of the ice and the gushing of the water, were the only sounds which reached the ears of the unfortunate Christlieb, who seemed to hear in the bells his death-knell, as his destruction was apparently inevitable. He had fallen upon his knees on the ice, which every moment became more the prey of the water as it rushed on. The town, his second home, and the place of many hopes, swam before his eyes; fainter became the sound of the bells, and darker appeared to him every object, while he heard the most dreadful noises in his ears. As often as the piece of ice on which he knelt shook beneath him from some fresh concussion, he thought his last moment had come. He pictured to himself the grief of his foster-father, the sorrow of Malchen, and the pity which Rupel would feel for his untimely end, and in this dreadful way. At length his senses became dulled, and he was unconscious of the cold of the ice water, in which he was covered up to his knees. He felt a drowsiness creep over him, and he shut his eyes, no longer looking at the desolation around him, until again awakened from his torpor by a new crashing of the ice.

Slowly he opened his weary eyes, and saw by the dim morning light, which was now struggling with the darkness of night, some dark arches suspended over the river. It was the bridge of the city, against whose stone pillars the huge blocks of ice were dashed, and driven back with a fearful noise. Lights were seen glimmering, and again reflected in the rushing waters. But Christlieb saw not that nets were placed between the pillars, in order to save any unhappy persons who might be driven down on the ice. The sight of the lights, however, recalled Christlieb to a sort of consciousness; for where lights are men are not generally far distant, and some one might perhaps yet save him. At all events, the bridge would decide his fate as soon as the piece of ice dashed against the pillars; and most likely it will be death, thought Christlieb The drums still were hanging on him; and they might now be the means of saving him. He was yet at a short distance from the bridge, and the mass of ice was floating slowly down, so that he was enabled to take off the drums from his person and beat an alarm, though with benumbed fingers. He likewise exerted all his remaining strength to utter a cry, but to no purpose, as far as he could see; for he now drove right against one of the stone pillars; the ice broke in two, and the larger half sunk beneath the water; the drums disappeared, and Christlieb, whose cry of agony was unheard, followed after them. He felt the rush of the water over his face, and a sharp pain in his side; after which his senses forsook him, and he was unconscious of what happened.

CHAPTER X.

THE SICK-BED.

How long Christlieb had remained unconscious, he knew not; neither could he very well tell whether he were in this world or in another. It seemed to him as if he were floating in mist, where huge shadows of men were flying past him. Then his head turned round and round, and he shut his eyes not to see anything more. Afterwards he became, as he thought, a receiver of the dead,--a post which certainly imagination alone could create. A large churchyard spread itself out before him, covered with snow, above which were seen the black crosses and stone monuments of the dead. At the entrance of the churchyard stood the house for the reception of the dead, where, however, Christlieb did not dwell, but hovered over it in the air, and saw the funeral processions of those of whom he was to take care move on to a distance. He likewise fancied that he had received a message from his late master, begging him to return to the tower, at the folly of which he smiled, as he knew that he was now no longer an inhabitant of earth. He felt himself quite happy, and had no desire to return to it again. The scene then changed, and he fancied himself standing up to the neck amidst the chilling ice, and making desperate efforts to reach the shore. These efforts, however, were always rendered unavailing by the united strength of two men and a lady, who kept him back, and pressed him seemingly deeper into the icy water. At length, after repeated struggles to get free, but all in vain, the blocks of ice changed themselves into bed-posts and bedding, under the latter of which he was covered, almost to suffocation. At another time he felt himself sitting upright in bed, and obliged to swallow a spoonful of something tasting like camphor or musk. Then, again, after long unconsciousness, he awoke and looked around him with open eyes. He saw a figure lying on a sofa at a short distance from him, with its head resting as if asleep. A small lamp was burning behind an open book, whose dim light was scarcely sufficient to light up the room, so as to render the objects distinctly visible. In another corner crackled a fire, which was blazing in a stove. Christlieb quietly left his bed, and with difficulty reached the door of the room, from the opening of which a cool air met him. At this moment the sleeping figure started up with a cry of horror, seized the weak and fainting boy, and brought him back again to his bed. When he next awoke a subdued daylight filled the apartment. A tall man stood beside him, holding his hand; and a beautiful, though pale, lady sat on the edge of his bed, to whom the doctor said, in a consoling tone of voice, "Madam, he is now out of danger. The fever has abated, and there only remains a debility and weakness quite natural after so severe an illness. Great care, however, is still necessary, with strict attention to all I have prescribed; for his nervous system is much shaken, and any relapse might be serious." Observing that the patient was awake, he said to him, "Dear Balduin, how do you find yourself?"

Not having heard the changed name, Christlieb replied cordially, "Thank you, I am very well."

At these words the countenance of the lady brightened up. "Do you know me again, my dear son?" she hastily asked Christlieb, bending over him, and looking at him with the greatest tenderness.

Christlieb gazed steadily at the unknown lady, and then shook his head as much as to say, No; which threw the lady into a state of great distress.

"Do not mind this," said the doctor; "it will be all right by and by. In nervous fevers, the memory, generally speaking, suffers most."

The lady was again comforted, and paid the greatest attention to the various orders which the doctor gave her, previous to his leaving, regarding the future treatment of the invalid. Meanwhile Christlieb took a survey of the apartment, which was like a palace compared to his former domicile. The walls were richly papered. The curtains of the windows were of silk; and the floor was covered with thick and elegant carpet. The furniture, tables, chairs, bed, and other articles, were of a brown, shining wood,--the tea-cups of painted china,--the spoons of pure silver. A beautiful embroidered bell-rope, with a handsome gilt handle, hung close to his bed;--the latter being somewhat softer and more elastic than his straw pallet in the tower. When he turned his look upon himself, he perceived that his night-dress was of the finest materials, his linen of the most expensive kind. Of his former dress, not a remnant was to be seen, while a splendid dressing-gown hung on the wall, and a pair of handsome worked slippers stood near his bed,--all evidently intended for him. Most gladly would he have asked where he was but his courage failed him.

After the lady had returned from taking leave of the doctor, she again sat down near the bed of the invalid, and began to knit, regarding him, every now and then, with an expression of the greatest affection. Christlieb felt much embarrassed. He wished exceedingly for a glass of water, yet did not like to ask the grand-looking lady for it. At length the latter, of her own accord, asked him if he would not like something to drink.

With profound respect, he answered, "If you will have the goodness, madam."

The lady immediately brought him a most refreshing drink, which Christlieb drank up, without leaving a single drop.

"I thank you very much," said he gratefully, which brought tears into the beautiful eyes of the lady. Afterwards she gave him a spoonful of medicine, which he patiently swallowed, though it was not much to his taste. He was far better pleased with the delicious apples, which, nicely roasted, and sprinkled with sugar, and along with a small biscuit, he was given at ten o'clock for his breakfast.

With great delight the lady saw him eat them, and never left the room until he had fallen into a gentle sleep, from which he did not awake until after noon. His watchful attendant was again there, and brought him a strengthening soup, placed him right in his bed, pushing pillows behind his back to keep him from falling, and from getting cold. When the lady saw her charge, with a steady hand, hold and use the spoon, and able to take the nourishing food, she exclaimed, in joyful accents, "Oh! how much your father will be delighted when he returns and finds you so well!"

"My father! my father!" said Christlieb, in evident confusion, and rubbing his forehead. In a moment the remembrance of the lost drums flashed on his memory, and he cried out, "Ah me! unfortunate one that I am; what will my master say about the drums?" Saying these words, as if in great distress, he let the spoon fall out of his hand.

The lady trembled with fear, dreading, from his confused words, that her patient was going to have a relapse. She was scarcely able to stammer out, "My dear Balduin, compose yourself. Throw all your cares and fears away. No one will be permitted to reproach you. Everything is already arranged."

But poor Christlieb could not be so easily comforted; and on this account, the sleep which he fell into towards evening was so light, that he heard all that passed between the doctor and his supposed mother.

"Ah!" she sighed, "my heart is torn between hope and fear, joy and sorrow! Since his illness, Balduin seems quite changed. He is no longer imperious, obstinate, disobedient, and discontented. He takes his medicine without one word of complaint; and for every morsel of bread, or draught of water, expresses thanks. Then, again, it makes me wretched when I think that, perhaps, his mind is affected, and that a settled form of insanity, or---- I cannot give utterance to such horrid fears. Yet the same idea which has possession of him when delirious from fever, seems to follow him when he is awake and tranquil."

Christlieb did not hear what answer the doctor made, as his sleep became deeper.

Next morning he had tea and cakes to breakfast; and he was so hungry, that he felt as if he could eat he knew not how many rolls. A servant helped him to put on the fine dressing-gown and slippers; and he was supported by her to the large easy chair, in which he rested, and enjoyed the mild rays of the sun, which likewise tempted the little birds to chirp and sing. Beside him stood his supposed mother, who said to him, as the servant was arranging his bed, "Do you not then love me, Balduin?"

"Oh! very much," replied Christlieb, blushing. "You are so kind to me, and I know not why I am thus treated."

"Do not speak to me in this way," said the lady; "but as you used to do. You are still my son, and my only joy."

"Ah! me," replied Christlieb humbly. "I am only a poor lad, and not worthy to be called your son."

"Speak not thus, my son," answered the lady. "It is true that by your former conduct you have caused both your father and myself much sorrow. When you left us, taking with you a considerable sum of money to riot with evil companions, then, it is true, we despaired of you. Still our affection made us hope that you might yet return to the right path; therefore your father, accompanied by your kind master, set off in search of you to bring you back if they found you. How will he be surprised when he finds his lost and erring son here, a changed and amended person! You are still our son, and now worthy of the name. Affliction, and the nearness of a fearful death have changed you, and given you back to yourself a new being. From the poverty of your dress, and from what escaped you when delirious, we have learnt how miserable you were when the money was all spent, and when your false friends forsook you. Now you will be able to appreciate the difference between your father's house, and wandering about with strangers. Twice have you been taken from us in a fearful way. Twice have you been miraculously restored to us."

Christlieb supposed that he must be again under the influence of the fever, and again delirious, when he heard these incomprehensible words of the lady. He looked strangely at her, and she seemed to regret what she had said, for she immediately changed the subject, asking Christlieb, with the greatest solicitude, if there was anything he would like to have, or any person he would like to see.

Christlieb was at no loss as to what he wished for, and the persons he most earnestly desired to behold; but this, perhaps, would be impossible, and was too much to expect. He fell into a reverie, and said nothing.

"Speak to me," repeated the lady kindly.

"I should like to have a violin," at length stammered out her patient.

"A violin!" said the lady in great amazement. "Very well, you shall have one when you are a little stronger; but at present you would hardly be able to hold it, or to draw the bow; besides, I fear that its harsh tones might be injurious to your nerves. Therefore you had better wait a short time before you get it."

The lady now assisted him back to his bed; but in doing so, he made a gesture as if in great pain.

"Is there anything the matter with you?" asked his affectionate nurse anxiously.

"I feel a pain in my side," replied Christlieb.

"Ah! I must have touched the part which was wounded by the fisherman when he drew you out of the water with his hook," said the lady.

Several days passed away, and with them Christlieb regained strength and health, to the delight of his affectionate nurse, who requested that he would call her mother as formerly. Christlieb promised to do so, but often forgot his part. As the lady most carefully abstained from all reference to past events, she had now no longer any misgivings about her patient's state of mind; but, in order to see whether he still remembered his lately expressed wish, she surprised him one day by the gift of a beautiful violin.

Christlieb's eyes sparkled at the sight of it, and the lady could not refrain from smiling when she saw the supposed Balduin take it in his hand. She, however, looked rather more serious when she perceived how well he seemed to know how to tune the instrument, how master-like he used the bow, and touched the strings. Her surprise increased every moment; and when he had played softly and with wonderful execution the thema of Rhode's variations, it had reached its zenith. When he had played one or two of the variations, his fingers and his bow becoming animated and full of fire, the amazed lady exclaimed, almost out of her senses, "Stop! you are not my Balduin; and yet you are my son! Had I not twins, and were they not both stolen, while only *one* was miraculously restored to me? You are my Reinhold, my gentler, dearer child!" She threw her arms around Christlieb, while the violin fell sounding from his hands on the floor.

CHAPTER XI.

THE MISTAKE.

In the public-house of a small town, situated at the foot of a hill, there sat four young men one sunny morning round a table, on which were placed wine bottles, rolls of wheaten bread, and Swiss cheese. They talked loudly and merrily, every few minutes emptying their glasses, which were plentifully supplied with golden wine. Their jests and laughter showed that they had rather swallowed too much of the exciting liquid. Except the person who waited on them, there was no one else in the room. The two principal speakers soon observed that their fourth companion sat leaning his head on his hand, and was lost in thought. One of them immediately bawled out, "Is the pet of his mother dying with home-sickness, that he sits there so miserable and whining?"

The youth who was thus addressed changed his posture, looked up and said, with a forced smile, "I am not troubled with home-sickness; but my purse is, in which there are now only four dollars. When these are finished, you will be good enough to open *your* treasures."

This speech made an unpleasant impression on the half-stupified wine-bibbers. Their faces became at once grave, and, in a most sober voice, one of them said, "Why did you not tell us this before? Had we known that the money of which you bragged so much was such a paltry sum, we would have thought twice about it before we became the companions of your expedition, and brought ourselves into disgrace with our guardians and tutors."

"Who incited me more to act as I have done than yourself, Nicholas?" asked the other in an angry voice. "It was you who advised me to borrow the money in the name of my father, and told us how to obtain false passports for our journey."

"Do not scold," drawled out a third; "but rather fight at once. When the money is done, then the comedy is ended! But you, Balduin, you must bear the blame. Crawl back to your parents, give them a few good words, and be our scape-goat; then the affair is finished, which, after all, is only a caprice of genius."

"Let us drink to our scape-goat Balduin," they all laughingly cried, raising at the same time their glasses to their lips. Balduin, to escape their mirth and scornful jests, thrust his head out of the window, while the others took good care that not one morsel of the breakfast should be left.

At this moment an aged man and a young girl entered the room in the dress of peasants. After a polite greeting, which was, however, only returned by the person who waited, the two travellers seated themselves on a bench near the door, and laid down their bundles.

"Bring us some bread and cheese," said the old man to the waiter, who immediately supplied him with what he asked. "There, Malchen, take and eat something; you will be much the better of it after our long journey this morning." Before the maiden complied with this request, she broke a small piece of the bread into crumbs, and then put her hand into a little bag, from which she drew forth a starling, who, delighted to escape from its prison, hopped about, and picked up the bread from the table. The young peasant, stroking the bird with her hands, said, "To-day you will see your old master. How pleased he will be to see you again!"

"And, it is to be hoped, still better pleased to see us," said the old man, "when he hears that we have come to live near him. I am not anxious about you, for you have learnt to work and to be useful; besides, town people generally prefer a servant-girl from the country. As to myself, I am sure God will not let me want; and when I have Christlieb again near me, I will fast gladly."

The young gentleman named Balduin now drew in his head from the window, and sat down at the table beside the others. He was seated with his back to the two strangers, yet in a moment they both recognised him, and almost screamed for joy. Our friend Kummas motioned with his hand to his companion to be quiet; and wishing to give, as he thought, his dear Christlieb a pleasant surprise, he advanced on tiptoe towards the table, giving the others a hint to say nothing, and suddenly placed his hard hands over the eyes of the sullen Balduin, saying in a feigned voice, "Who am I?"

"No nonsense!" cried Balduin, seeking to free his face from its unwelcome covering. But Kummas held his hands firm as a vice, repeating in tones trembling with pleasure, "Who is it?" The supposed Christlieb, in a passion, tore away the hands of the old man from his face, and sprang from his seat. "What do you mean by this impertinence?" asked Balduin enraged, while Kummas took hold of him and said, "It is your foster-father, dear Christlieb; and here is Malchen,"----

"And your starling, too!" continued the young girl, weeping with joy.

The three young idlers at this broke out into a loud scornful laugh.

"Brother dear, we congratulate you on your new relations, not forgetting the starling. Ha! ha! ha!"

Balduin drove the old man from him with violence, and paid no heed to Malchen. "You vagabonds," he cried, "you will pay dearly for your insolent jest!"

Kummas stood petrified; he raised his arms, and then let them fall down powerless. At length he found strength to say, "Christlieb! are we really so much changed that you do not know us? I am Kummas, this is Malchen, whose grandfather is dead, and we are going to the town in which you live."

"Now I hope you understand!" again shouted Balduin's rude companions. "Such a father is not found every day on the street, neither such a smart young peasant girl."

Balduin trembled with passion. "You must have escaped from Bedlam!" he cried; "away with you! You will get nothing from me!"

The old man could scarcely believe his ears. "No, it is impossible," he said to himself, "that within the short space of one year an angel could be thus changed into a demon. Christlieb!" he continued, "dissemble no longer; you are breaking my heart with your jokes. I have not deserved this treatment; but I need not speak of what I have done for you, as you have always gratefully acknowledged it."

Instead of answering, Balduin paid the reckoning, and left the inn with his noisy companions, leaving Kummas and Malchen behind, who both stood as if rooted to the spot.

A long pause ensued. "Is he really gone?" asked Kummas, scarcely able to speak.

"Quite gone!" Malchen was only able to answer by a sorrowful shake of the head.

"He has denied us, Malchen!" said the old man. "He is in prosperity, as you may see by his dress and well-filled purse. He has been ashamed of us before the other scholars. Alas! alas! I was not ashamed, for his sake, to become like an old nurse." Kummas laid down his head and wept bitterly. "See," he continued after a time, "how soon our soap bubbles have burst! Now we may return the way we came to our old home in the village. You will be able to get something to do; perhaps to herd the cows or the geese; and I---- will find a grave. The ingratitude of my child will be my winding-sheet! What could I now do with a violin? Never again shall I handle the bow, and I will burn the instrument as I did the violincello in which---- Christlieb was cradled." He again laid his grey head on the table, which became wet with his burning tears.

Malchen sprang up in haste. "Father! father!" she cried, "look at the starling." The poor bird lay with its breast bruised flat, close to the table where the young men had been drinking. His supposed master had accidentally put his foot on it when he had jumped up in rage at the old man.

"Father!" said Malchen, weeping, and holding the poor little thing by its legs, "the starling is dead!"

Kummas looked up. "It has been treated like me," he said with indifference. "The starling is only a senseless bird; but me has my child killed. Oh! that I, too, were dead!"

CHAPTER XII.

THE UNEXPECTED DISCOVERY.

Some time elapsed before Kummas found himself able to resume his journey. The bread and cheese remained untouched, which, however, Malchen put into her basket; and the starling, yet warm, she again placed in her bag. They went a long way without speaking; at length Kummas broke the silence--"I now believe," said he, "that it was Christlieb who destroyed your grandfather's nets! Who could have thought him such a liar, unless to-day we had had the most convincing proof of it! So it would appear there is no knowing people; not even if we do eat a bushel of salt with them! Who is to be trusted?"

"Trust me," said Malchen confidently.

"You!" replied Kummas, smiling in bitterness of feeling. "Why, I would have built houses on Christlieb,"----

"And on me too, father, and bridges into the bargain," continued Malchen. "You must not take it amiss if I say that perhaps you have been too hasty in turning back. The wine may have affected Christlieb; and if he had been alone he might have spoken differently."

"'Drunken words, true words,' says the proverb," answered Kummas; "and had I been a king, and Christlieb only a cowherd, would I have been ashamed of him? His comrades, the young players, are no better than we are! Am I not a musician as well as they? If Christlieb is already so proud, what will he be when he becomes a Paganini? It would have been my greatest joy if I could have taken my place behind him and said,--See, I took this Paganini out of a manger, and brought him up in a violincello!"

"He will come to his senses again," whispered Malchen, "when he has had his own way for a time."

"No, no; he must be a demon to have acted as he has done," replied the much injured Kummas.

"Don't speak in this wicked way, father!" rejoined the young girl; "have you no longer a spark of love for your Christlieb?"

The old man stood still, strove with his feelings for a few minutes, and then said more mildly, "God forgive me! I am too severe; and yet I mean it not in earnest. Yes, Malchen, I would joyfully give up my life, if by so doing I could make Christlieb what he was, although he has broken my heart."

They soon came to the town where they had rested the previous night, and which was now all bustle and confusion,--it being the day of the yearly fair.

With difficulty the wanderers pressed through the moving crowd. As they turned the corner of a street close to the market-place, they met a man and his wife, the former blind, and playing on a pipe; the latter, whose countenance was the colour of copper and much swollen, was playing on a barrel organ, accompanying it with her screeching voice.

Kummas started at the sight of them. "Look!" he said to Malchen, "that miserable pair might have been sitting comfortably in a warm house had they acted properly. The blind man was the landlord of a small inn in the village of Toumern, where I often used to play. His wife drank up everything, and brought herself and her husband to begging. They are called Hicup."

While Malchen was looking at the man and woman a scene occurred, not at all unusual in such places and at such times. A rather aged woman, carrying on her bent back a small raree-show, pushed her way into the midst of the throng, where the two wretched musicians had taken up their quarters; and here, by the assistance of a companion who was along with her, the show was lifted from her back, and arranged for the benefit of the idle and curious passers by. This attracted the notice of dame Hicup, who, seeing her domain invaded, began most furiously to abuse the woman, when a serious quarrel took place. In the progress of the squabble our former hostess of the nether inn was somehow or the other enlightened in a way about her rival, which quite changed the character of her abusive epithets. In order to be the more able for her work, dame Hicup left her tambourine on the top of the organ, and advanced to the show-woman with arms a-kimbo. "So you have given up the crockery and stoneware trade!" she shouted to her antagonist in the fine arts. "Have you not another pair of brats to give me? I can tell you where one of the two is which you left with me fifteen years since. He is now a beer-fiddler, and may help you to earn your bread. He can play while you exhibit your trumpery pictures. Bless me! is that you, Kummas? I will now confess that I put your Christlieb in the manger at the door of the inn, from which you took him out and carried him home. If I had known that you were so fond of children, I would have given you the other young one too, his brother. They were as like as two drops of water. You may thank this woman for your foundling, and ask her where she got them. It was easy to be seen they were not her own, the thief that she is! Oh, you child-stealer!" she shouted to the woman with the show, who turned pale, and quickly disappeared, leaving the field to her victorious enemy. Seeing this, dame Hicup redoubled her abuse and her scolding; and her shouting soon collected a mob, from the midst of which Kummas and Malchen could scarcely make their way out, as they thought they had heard enough to enable them to regulate their future movements.

When Kummas had recovered from the surprise which the conversation of the woman had caused, he turned to Malchen and said, "Did you hear,

Malchen, that Christlieb had a brother who was his very counterpart? Might the gay-looking youngster we saw this morning not have been he, while the real Christlieb is still in the tower? My Christlieb had no mole on his left temple, and I think that jackanapes had."

"Now," replied Malchen, "there can be no doubt as to the person who let the birds of my grandfather escape, and destroyed the nets."

"Come, then, let us retrace our steps," said Kummas, in a more cheerful voice. "It is fortunate we were no further away. I would not have missed the hearing of this quarrel for all the treasures in the world." In spite of weariness, Kummas stepped briskly on, while Malchen skipped merrily after him. Even the dead starling was for the moment forgotten.

The quarrel of the two women had not been without important results. The magistrates had thought it incumbent on them to interfere, and both vagrants were taken to prison. In the course of evidence the truth was not, however, altogether brought out, as the old woman stoutly maintained the children to be those of her daughter, who had been long dead; but confessed that she had left them in the house of dame Hicup. The further examination of the prisoners was therefore deferred until various inquiries had been instituted, and notices of the case put into all the public papers. Meanwhile Christlieb lay ill in the house of the director of the police at the capital, whose owner, in company with his son's tutor, Mr. Werter, was searching for the runaway Balduin. Kummas, followed by Malchen, was making the best of his way towards the small town in which dwelt the leader of the town-band, where Christlieb was expected to be found.

CHAPTER XIII.

THE BAD RECEPTION.

Balduin and his companions had reached the same town. This happened the very day after Christlieb had been taken to the capital, towards which he had been driven by the memorable event of the breaking up of the ice. The river was still here and there covered with huge pieces of ice, while it had far overflowed its banks. The young adventurers, with many others, stood on the edge of the stream looking at its singular appearance.

"There must be a beautiful view from the tower up there," thought Balduin, as he pointed to poor Christlieb's late abode. "Who will come with me up the long staircase, and see what is to be seen?"

"As we have nothing better to do, we may as well all accompany you," said one of his companions; and they quickly walked in the direction of the cathedral. They passed a baker's shop on their way, which another of them perceiving, exclaimed, "I am sure the view will be seen to much more advantage if we are provided with some cakes or biscuits. Give me the rest of your money, Balduin; and if you will go up and find the best place for us to have a view from, we will follow directly with something nice to eat, and a small bottle of cordial." He gave the other two youths a most significant wink, which they were at no loss to comprehend. Balduin completely emptied his now scanty purse, gave all he had to his faithless friends, and began to ascend the steps of the tower.

"Now, my good fellows, it is high time for us to beat a retreat!" shouted the false friend to whom Balduin had given the money. "We must go back to our tutors and make them believe that we have repented of our doings, and left our leader Balduin, in order not to be corrupted by his wicked society. As I said to-day already, Balduin shall be our scape-goat; we have had a merry life this last fortnight at his expense."

The others agreed; purchased some cakes to eat on the road, and at once began their homeward journey.

Almost breathless, Balduin reached the top of the steps, and rung the bell at the shut door of the *stadt-musikus*, which was opened to him by the servant girl. "Bless me!" she exclaimed in joyful surprise, "is that you, Master Christlieb? Where have you come from? And where have you got the fine clothes? I scarce would have known you, you are so changed. What will the master and mistress say, who have been in such a way about their kettledrums? We were afraid that, last night, you had been on the ice when it broke up so suddenly, and that you were drowned."

Balduin looked very stupid at this unexpected harangue. "I am surely bewitched!" he muttered to himself. He turned round to descend the steps, not in the best humour, when he was prevented by the appearance of Mr. Dilling, Mrs. Dilling, and all the scholars, who had heard the exclamation of the servant, and came out to see Christlieb, and to hear what happened to him.

"Where have you the kettledrums?" asked the town musician in a voice of thunder, looking very suspiciously at Balduin's fine dress. "Sold, pawned, made away with, I have no doubt!" seizing as he said this, the petrified Balduin by the neck.

"Where are the drums?" screamed the angry lady, shaking her clenched hand in his face.

"Where are the drums?" echoed the malicious boys, delighted at the embarrassment and distress of their companion.

"The drums!" stammered out Balduin, his lips quivering with passion.--"What do I----?"

"Yes, the drums! the drums!" bellowed out Mr. Dilling, accompanying his words with blows and pinches of the ear. "I will have my drums, which cost thirty-six dollars, and twenty groschens. I say, where are they? Where have you got these fine clothes? Are not my drums pawned for them?"

"Let the boy speak, Mr. Dilling," said Rupel, gently.--"He may be quite innocent. In consequence of the breaking up of the ice, he perhaps was prevented crossing the river last night, and had to walk all the way to the capital to cross the bridge; then to come here; and how could he carry the heavy drums all that long way? Most likely he has left them at the inn where the concert was."

"But where has he got the fine clothes?" said Mr. Dilling in a less angry tone.

"That I know not," answered Rupel; "Christlieb himself will be able to explain it all, I am sure; only let him speak."

"Where are my drums?" asked now Mr. Dilling in a composed voice.--"Speak, and tell me where you got these fine clothes!"

"These clothes are my own property," replied Balduin haughtily; "and as for your drums, I know nothing about them."

Scarcely were these words uttered, when the *stadt-musikus*, more enraged than ever, flew at the unfortunate speaker, and began to beat him without mercy. In vain poor Balduin attempted to speak, in vain he tried to defend himself. Even Rupel's remonstrances were not listened to in the midst of the uproar.

Such treatment had the over-indulged Balduin never before received. He was stunned, stupified, and, for the first time in his life, afraid. Whenever he opened his lips to offer some explanation, he was stopped by Mr. Dilling thundering out, "Silence, sir!" and raising his hand to give him another blow. Balduin anxiously awaited the arrival of his three companions, in the hope that they would extricate him from his unpleasant situation; but poor Balduin waited in vain. He seated himself in a corner of the room, weeping bitterly from pain and anger, while the enraged master gave vent to the remainder of his wrath in scolding words.--"I would have the rascal arrested," he continued, after a volley of abusive epithets; "did I not need him to-day; indeed I cannot do without him at the concert which is to take place in the town, and at which he is to play the oboe. Come along, we have no time to lose; evening will soon be here, and as yet we have no rehearsal; all on account of that worthless fellow. Make haste!"

The music-stands were immediately set up, the instruments in the hands of the pupils, and the miserable Balduin shown where he was to take his place. When the oboe was thrust into his hand by one of the boys, he exclaimed, "But, indeed, I cannot----"

"Is he again daring to speak?" cried Mr. Dilling, taking hold of a stick, and threatening to strike him.--"You are there, sir, to blow, and not to reason."

In despair, Balduin took the instrument, and, after a few unsuccessful attempts, raised the mouthpiece of the oboe to his lips, and placed himself before the music-stand. The overture began, and Balduin blew as if his cheeks would crack; when suddenly an evil spirit seemed to have taken possession of the town musician. Purple with rage, he sprung from his place and struck the unfortunate player a dreadful blow on the head, saying, "What wretched playing is that?--do you mean to make a fool of me?"

A stream of blood from Balduin's mouth was the only answer; and the concert speedily came to an end; for Balduin fell senseless into the arms of Rupel, who came to his aid. From the violence of the blow the under end of the oboe had struck against the music-stand, while the sharp point had pierced Balduin's throat.

"That is all pretence," stammered the now pale-faced master.--"Wife, give the lad something to gargle his throat with. There is very little the matter with him."

Balduin, however, soon showed that something serious was the matter. He gasped for breath as if in agony, and fresh streams of blood gushed from his mouth. His companions now all looked very grave, and there was an end of their jests. Rupel assisted the unhappy youth to his bed, and then went away without saying where he was going. When Mr. Dilling (who was rather alarmed at what had happened) missed him, he cried out, "Where has Rupel gone to?--Does he mean to make a noise about the matter? Is he no better than an idle chatterbox? I tell you what it is," turning to the others, "if any of you dare to say one word of this in the town, I will knock your heads off. I am tormented enough to-day by the loss of an *oboist*. The good-for-nothing scoundrel;--he is the cause of the whole disturbance."

The door-bell now rang. "Who is there?" asked Dilling, half out of his wits, as he pushed aside the servant and went to open the door himself. "What do you want?" he asked, in no gentle voice, the two strangers who presented themselves. "My tower is no dove-cot, and there is nothing to be had here."

"We do not want anything, sir," answered the honest Kummas; "we only come to visit my Christlieb Fundus, the little Paganini."

"Your Christlieb?" asked Dilling in a shaking voice. "And who are you, may I ask?"

"Christlieb is my foster-son; and, with your permission, I am the musician Kummas, from Gelenau. This is Malchen, the child of an old neighbour of mine who is dead; she sings like a lark. We have come a long way to see our Christlieb; so have the kindness to tell us where he is."

During this speech the unhappy Mr. Dilling stood as if on red-hot coals. Collecting all his strength he then muttered, "Truly, you sent me a fine specimen of a youth! The rascal has run away, pawned, or sold my kettledrums, to buy himself gay clothes. But I will bring him to the house of correction for this."

Kummas was as if struck by a second thunderbolt. He reeled backwards, and would have fallen, had not Malchen supported him. "Can this be true?" he said in a low voice to himself.--"Heaven have pity on me! is he really lost?-- lost beyond hope!" His head sank on Malchen's shoulder, and he stood mute as a statue.

Warring with his feelings, Mr. Dilling looked at the old man and his companion. He hemmed and coughed, but could not utter a word. At length Kummas said, in a voice of sadness, "And where is my former Christlieb, who now, it seems, neither regards God nor me?"

"How do I know?" replied the embarrassed town musician.--"I tell you he has ran away."

"Come, then, Malchen," said the old broken-hearted man; "I have now nothing to seek but a grave. There, in its stillness, I will rest my weary head; for I am desolate." With these words Kummas turned to go away, and Malchen, weeping, led him carefully and slowly down the steps from the tower. Dilling looked long after them irresolute; but the fear of blame shut his mouth, and he went back into the house, where, in his room, his wife and servant were busy washing away the marks of the blood. Half-way down the steps, Kummas paused to take breath near an open window. "Let me rest here a few minutes, Malchen; the fresh air may revive me." Both stood in silence; but without eyes for the beauty of the scene around them. After a short time they heard the voices and footsteps of persons ascending the staircase.

"I pray you, doctor, do all in your power for the youth," said one of the persons.--"He is the best player of us all."

"Which of them is it?" asked the other.

"It is Christlieb Fundus," replied the first speaker; "the best player on the violin. Show the master that there is some cause for alarm, so that he may not treat the matter as a trifle. I tell you, a stab from a dagger could not be worse than one from the sharp point of an oboe."

At the name of Christlieb, Kummas had become attentive to what was said. A ray of hope gleamed upon him, and he raised his head, awaiting, most anxiously, the appearance of the speakers, who, in a moment or two afterwards, reached the place where he was standing. He addressed them in a voice struggling with emotion. "Kind sirs," he began, "for the love of heaven, tell me where my son Christlieb Fundus is, and what is the matter with him? Has he really run away? or is he sick?"

A glance at the old man was sufficient to determine Rupel to speak the truth.

"If Christlieb is your child, then I will not disguise from you that he has received an injury, and is lying very ill in his bed. Your arrival, though not at the happiest time, is nevertheless fortunate."

"One word more," said Kummas, as Rupel and the doctor were hurrying past;--"is my son really so wicked as the master affirms?"

"The Master!" repeated Rupel, surprised, for he supposed that the two travellers were only on their way up.--"Your son has been always good and well-behaved, and in a single day he could not become the very reverse."

Kummas became less sad; as he would far rather his child were sick in body, than perverse in mind. Malchen and he soon reached again the top of the stairs, and were not long in seeing their favourite, whom they found already under the hands of the doctor, and in a most dangerous state. At this moment, neither of them thought of the mole on the left temple, nor of the fine clothes which were strewn about the room. Kummas and Malchen attended to all the wants of poor Balduin, who, unable to speak, could neither thank them nor unravel the mystery. He now passed through a severe school, which, however, became the means of his radical cure. For three long days he was unable to swallow anything, in consequence of his swollen throat. Afterwards, his medicine and a little tea had to be taken in drops. He was helpless as a child, and had it not been for his youthful strength, the care of the doctor, and the unremitting watchfulness of the old man and Malchen, he could not have recovered. He no longer refused their assistance, but gladly took from the hand of Malchen any cooling draught she offered. Their constant presence lessened the tediousness of the slow creeping hours. How could he have remained insensible to so much love,--to the self-denial exercised for his sake by two persons wholly unconnected with him! When Balduin's sleepless eye, sometimes, during the night, fell on the old man, who, overcome by sleep, was resting on his hard bed of straw, with a thin cover over him,--when he heard the loud regular stroke of the pendulum above his head, sounding as it seemed a death-knell, and saw by the glimmering light of the feeble lamp the black walls of the tower,--then came the elegant dwelling of his father, with all its luxuries, before the eye of his mind. He thought of his gentle mother, who had only been too indulgent to him, and whose heart, as well as that of his affectionate father, he had made sad by his ingratitude. He remembered the treachery and desertion of his three companions; and, overcome by a deep sense of his former thoughtlessness and guilt, he resolved from henceforth, to endeavour to be quite a different character. Remorse had touched his heart, his eyes were opened, and he prayed to God for forgiveness,--to that God who had long, by gentle and gracious means, sought to lead him into paths of virtue, but who now had seen it needful to teach him by affliction and adversity. Balduin, subdued and humbled, now enjoyed the peace which is above all price; and his bodily health amended with that of his mind.

CHAPTER XIV.

THE REUNION.

We often seek at a distance what is to be found quite at hand; and so it happened with Balduin's father, the director of police, Mr. von Winsing, who was searching for his runaway son in remote districts, while the youth was only some miles distant from the capital. A newspaper, which accidentally fell into his hands, made him hastily change his route. This was the notice (already mentioned as being inserted in the public papers) of the detention in prison of the two vagrants, dame Hicup and the woman with the show-box, with an account of the circumstances connected with their seizure. Only a matter of deep interest could have induced the sorrowful father to give up for a time the search of his son, as it was possible he might from what he had read obtain possession of the other child so long lost to him. When he arrived at the small town of Brixen, where the two women were imprisoned, he immediately went to the magistrate and made the following deposition:--

"My dear wife, in the second year of our marriage, presented me with two boys, fine healthy twins, and as like each other as two drops of water. Except by a very small mole on the left cheek of our youngest born, it was almost impossible to distinguish the one from the other. To our great joy they grew in health and strength until they were nine months old, when they were stolen from us in a manner as bold as it was shameless. The grown-up son of the nurse who had charge of the infants was a worthless fellow, and, in consequence of a serious crime he had committed, I was obliged by the duties of my office to have him arrested, and given over for punishment. His mother foolishly imagined that the fate of her son rested with me, and wept and entreated me to set him at liberty. As she failed in obtaining her desire by these means, she meditated a plan which might, as she thought, enable her to attain her object. The letter which she left behind stated that the only way of again receiving the children was to free her son, and to hold her as innocent. These were the only conditions on compliance with which our infants would be restored to us. In addition, the most fearful threats were used if we dared to send persons to find out her place of hiding, or if employed any means whatever for that purpose. We knew too well the unbending character of the woman; and as I had no power to turn aside the course of justice, we feared for the lives of our children. After mature reflection, I resolved to set out myself in search of the woman, and to be very wary and cautious in my proceedings, hoping that if I found her I might get my children by gentle means, or if not, by force. Giving myself no rest either by night or day, it was no wonder if one night I fell asleep in my carriage. But who can describe my astonishment when, at my awaking at daybreak, I saw by the grey light of morning, lying on the empty seat opposite, the youngest of my sons, distinguished by the mole on his left cheek. How he had come there, by whom brought, neither I nor the postilion could tell. So far my search had been fruitless; and it was now necessary, in consequence of this singular circumstance, to return home to my despairing wife. Fifteen long years passed away without our being able to obtain the slightest clue as to what had become of the other child. Permit me then, sir, to have an interview with both prisoners, that I may gain certain information of the life or death of my son. Indeed, I could almost wish to hear of the latter; for if our Balduin, brought up with such care, has caused us so much sorrow, how much worse may not our eldest born have become, falling--as in all probability he would do--into worthless hands."

"I am happy, my dear sir," replied the magistrate, "to have it in my power to allay your apprehensions on that point. You would see from the newspapers that the unfeeling dame Hicup, when she had put the one into the post carriage, placed the other in a manger, from which it was taken out by a poor fiddler, called Kummas, who adopted it. From inquiries we directed to be made in the village where the old man lived, the village of Gelenau, it was ascertained, both from the pastor and the schoolmaster, that your son had become a clever and an excellent youth, and that at present he was in the town of Waldau studying music with the master of the band in that place. It is likewise said that his foster-father, old Kummas, lately left the village, in order to go and live in the neighbourhood of his foster-son, to whom he is very much attached."

The two gentlemen now proceeded to visit the prisoners,--going, in the first instance, to examine the nurse who had stolen them. The moment this woman saw her former master enter the cell she became pale, and turned away her head. As the time for deception, however, was now past, with many tears she confessed what she had done.

"Hannah," said her master with much emotion, "how happy you might have been in your old age had you remained faithful to your trust; for we never would have seen the nurse of our children want for anything. But tell me, how did your son reward you after he came from the house of correction for the deed you had done for his sake?"

A painful expression passed over the face of the woman at this question; and she answered, in a tone of bitterness, "For my love he misused me, and deserted me."

"That is always the reward of the wicked," said the police director, "may it be your only punishment. But why did you leave the children with a stranger, rather than return them to their parents?"

"Hatred and dread of punishment," replied Hannah. "When I had wandered with them on my back for five days in woods and solitary places, I was unable to carry them any farther, so I determined to free myself of them in a proper way. Besides, I thought that if I were caught and put in prison, I might be the better able to make conditions by refusing to tell the place where I had left them, unless leniently dealt with."

Dame Hicup, into whose cell they next went, complained bitterly of the hardship of having been so long imprisoned, as she conceived that instead of being punished in this fashion, she deserved a recompense, as she had managed so well with the twins, and had been the means of discovering the real thief. The director of police promised to get her and her blind husband admission into a charitable institution, where they might lead a comfortable life, with the exception of brandy-drinking, as of that liquid they would find none. Mr. von Winsing had now nothing to do but hasten to Waldau, there to seek his son at the house of the *stadt-musikus*.

Reinhold, the son whom he expected to find there, was still in the capital with his mother, and perfectly restored to health. The Lady von Winsing had written to her husband relating the joyful tidings of having found her eldest-born: but, in consequence of the director's change of plan, the letter had not reached him. When Madame von Winsing, by a letter from Brixen, learnt what had happened, and where her husband had gone to, she resolved to give him a surprise by meeting him, along with Reinhold, at Waldau; and therefore made preparations for doing so. The chief thing to be done was to purchase a pair of kettle-drums, without which Christlieb declared he dared not face his former master.

Almost at the same hour when Mr. Winsing left Brixen for Waldau, his lady and Christlieb started from the capital for the same town.

Balduin, in the meanwhile, was so far recovered as to be able to walk on to the gallery to breathe the pleasant air of spring.

The *stadt-musikus*, whose selfishness returned as his fears departed, had this morning plainly told Kummas and Malchen that their presence was no longer necessary, and that they must now look out for some other lodging. He was, however, not a little surprised when Balduin told him that he was not Christlieb, but the son of the police director at the capital. Kummas and Malchen were not so much amazed, for they of late had begun to have their doubts, when they remembered the mole on the left cheek and the fine clothes. They did not regret what they had done from love to the apparent Christlieb; but they were oppressed with anxiety as to what had become of the real one. Without any hint from the town-musician, they had resolved to depart whenever they were assured that Balduin was not their Christlieb; and they immediately prepared for their departure to seek for their dear lost one.

In vain Balduin entreated them first to go with him to see his parents, as soon as the doctor thought him fit for the journey; nothing would keep them, no reward induce them to delay. As Malchen was tying up their few poor clothes, she whispered to Kummas, "Although Balduin certainly at first treated us very ill, yet I cannot help liking him, in spite too of his killing the poor starling; for he is so like Christlieb, and I think is far more reasonable than he was."

"You may be right as to the last part of your speech," replied the old man; "but not in the first. Master Balduin, with his pale face and sunk eyes, is only like the moon; but my Christlieb, with his rosy cheeks, is like the fiery sun; and even were that not the case, my Christlieb can play on the violin, while this Balduin can only whine."

The door bell rang, and Balduin's father stepped in when the servant opened. He seemed panting for breath; wiped the perspiration from his forehead, and then said, "Where is the town-musician? Are the pupils within?"

The maid-servant directed him to the small gallery where Dilling was walking, as well as Balduin. In spite of the paleness and thinness of Balduin (the effect of his illness), the police director instantly recognised his son. But, in order not to alarm him, he remained for a few moments looking at him. When, however, Balduin accidentally turned fully round his face, Mr. Winsing could resist no longer, and, rushing up to him with open arms, he exclaimed, "Yes; there can be no doubt! you are my son Reinhold! behold in me your father, dear child, and embrace me!"

Balduin had sunk on his knees before his deeply affected parent, and said, "Father, forgive me! I have erred and done wrong; but I have been grievously punished for my folly."

Here the *stadt-musikus* looked rather embarrassed and fidgetty, while the police director cried out in astonishment, "Are you not"----

"I am Balduin, your unworthy son, and not the gentle Christlieb, or Reinhold, who attracts all hearts," said the repentant youth.

"But where, then, is the real Christlieb?" asked the gentleman, turning to Mr. Dilling. "Was he not a pupil of yours, and his foster-father a poor village musician?"

"Where he is I know not," replied the *stadt-musikus*. "Since the breaking up of the ice he has disappeared, along with my kettle-drums."

"How dreadful!" exclaimed Mr. von Winsing. "Just at the moment when, after a fifteen years' separation, I had hoped to embrace my child, to hear that I may have lost him for ever."

At this moment the servant came and announced that a stranger wished to see Mr. Dilling, who, glad to make his escape, hastened away. Balduin meanwhile related to his father everything that had happened to him, and all he had suffered.

The town-musician was most agreeably surprised when a man laden with two superb kettle-drums, stood before him. "Master Christlieb Fundus sends his respects," stammered out the man, "and sends you back your drums. Not the old drums, to be sure, for they were lost in the river; but speck and span new ones.--Master Christlieb begs you will excuse their not having been sent sooner; but he has been long very ill." With these words, the messenger put down the shining drums, with their snow-white leather tops and elegant sticks, which the town musician most joyfully received. His delight was augmented when the door again opened, and Christlieb himself, followed by his mother, walked into the house, and rushed into the arms of old Kummas, whom he encountered ready for his departure.

"Hurrah!" exclaimed the old man, shedding tears of joy, while he pressed his foster-son to his heart; "this is the real Christlieb! Rejoice with me, for I have again found my Fundus!"

"Mother! dearest mother!" sobbed Christlieb, "this is my good foster-father, who took me out of the manger, and carried me in the violincello to his home."

The high-bred, beautiful lady most heartily embraced the honest countryman, while Christlieb went on to say,--"Father Kummas, this is my mother, the kindest-hearted person in all the world; and there is Malchen," he continued, still more pleased, drawing the bashful girl forward; "Malchen, the faithful friend, who brought me the cake when I was in the dungeon, and who took care of my starling!"

"And here is your excellent father," said Madame von Winsing, hastening towards her husband, who had just entered the room. "Oh! my dear husband, what a son have we found in Reinhold!"

His father embraced the latter in a tumult of joy. "Seeing, however, poor Balduin weeping in a corner, who did not presume to mingle with the happy circle, Mr. von Winsing turned towards him and took him by the hand to lead him to his mother.

"Dear wife," said the director, "this tower is an enchanted place! It makes the sorrowful glad and the wicked good. Our Balduin has lately had some lessons here, which have quite changed him. He is now worthy of your affection."

Mr. Dilling had been all this time in a fever of anxiety to try his new drums, and now he could resist no longer. Without being asked, he began, by a splendid flourish on them, to play the sublime melody of--

"Now let us all thank God!"

And to this every one present responded with profound feelings of gratitude.

THE END.

THE WOOD-GATHERER

One summer evening, a girl, barefoot and clad in a ragged frock, might have been seen in a deep wood, gathering fuel. She was scarcely ten years old, yet for a long time had been sent out by her parents, day after day, to seek, as now, dry sticks, or, if it was spring-time, rampions and wild hops, or, if it were summer, strawberries and hillberries, and to offer these for sale from house to house.

When she had nothing to sell, she had to go about begging. Without bringing something she dared not return home, if she wished to escape a scolding, or even being beaten; for her parents were poor, and her father a moody and passionate man.

It had not always been so; but since unproductive times and repeated recurrence of sickness in his family had prevented him from advancing, as he had hoped, in his trade--he was a shoemaker--he had, under a godless dejection, given himself up to drinking, thereby scaring away his last customers, and completing his domestic misery.

The mother, a capital wife, as one would say, but as little acquainted with God and His Word as her husband, was thenceforth compelled to bear singly the burden of supporting her family, and was accustomed to go out and earn money by washing. For more than a year the sorely-smitten family had been deprived even of this scanty means of subsistence, the poor woman's uninterrupted exertions by day and by night having brought on a severe illness, and laid her paralytic--lame, hand and foot--in bed, surrounded by her raging husband, and the three half-naked and starving children.

The eldest of the children was Mary, our wood-gatherer.

The little girl, as she is to be met to-day deep in the wood, has collected a pretty large bundle of dry branches, but is weary from her long wandering about the bushes, and lays herself down to rest on the moss-grown roots of a tall, shady beech-tree.

And while she sits, it is as if the birds in the wood all found an inward compassion with the poor child, and would, as far as lay in their power, encourage, comfort, and cheer her.

Our little Mary thought within herself that she had never heard the feathered songsters sing so sweetly as they were now doing in choirs on the green twigs around her.

And it was indeed delightful to listen how the finch warbled here in short, fresh lay, and the titmouse and sisken there sounded their tender notes; and how, from the copse threaded by the brook, arose the long-breathed farewell song of the nightingale; and, from the far distance, the full melancholy trill of the blackbird floated touchingly over.

The cuckoo, also, and the turtle-dove, gave their contribution to the general concert; the ravens, also, in the neighbouring oak, to whom the song is denied, appeared desirous of contributing their share to the entertainment of the little maid, and fed their young before her eyes, and the young ones stretched their necks out of the high nest, and opened wide their bills. The squirrels frisked about, now here, now there, and leaped from tree to tree; and many of the birds came close to Mary's feet, and picked up worms, or a feather, or flock of moss, and flew away with it to their nests.

Mary looked a long time at this joyous life almost with adoration; and, in the still, lofty wood, her heart had a strange feeling, as if she could, at the same time, laugh and weep. She had also her own thoughts, glad and sorrowful, but more of the latter, and yet she did not herself very well know what she really thought. At last she bent her head on her breast, and the evening zephyrs sighed her asleep.

During the slumber she had a wonderful dream.

She dreamed that she was again in a deep lonely wood, and as she looked up, see! there walked through the shades of the trees, clothed in a shining white garment, a majestic form with a friendly countenance.

All the birds immediately gathered round the mysterious man, and hovered about him with wonderful songs, the like of which she had never heard. And from his full hands he strewed food of all kinds for the cheerful singers, and the birds picked it up, and carried it to their nests, and flew back singing still more heartily and beautifully than before.

And Mary heard the name of the gracious man distinctly repeated in every chorus, and it seemed as if she had never heard so sweet and dear a name. And Mary thought--"Oh, thou kind man, were I but one of these kind birds of thine, and wert thou but to step once into our cottage as thou enterest here!"

And as she thus thought, she was just on the point of rising to hasten after him, and seize the hem of his garment, and say, "Not so, you come to us also;" but then she awoke, and, alas! what she had heard and seen was but a dream. She found herself alone in the dark wood, for the sun had long ago gone down. By her side lay the bundle of sticks--nothing more. Deep silence reigned around her, only broken by the rustling of the evening wind among the leaves of the trees, and now and then the solitary doleful sounds which were winged across from the distant nightingales, and now and then a beetle humming in the air, or a glow-worm shining amongst the shrubs.

Sorrowfully Mary rose up from her mossy seat, put her faggot on her shoulders, and took the way home.

But the sensations kindled by the pleasant dream lived on in her heart, and the image of the friendly man had impressed itself indelibly on her mind.

If she could but recall his name! In her dream it was repeatedly and distinctly pronounced in the songs of the birds, but at the moment of awaking it had escaped, and, cast about as she might, it was not again to be found.

This is not to be wondered at. All over Christendom there are still houses like those of the heathens, where the name in which all salvation is contained is unknown, or, if known, unpronounced.

Such a house that of the parents of this poor child unfortunately was. Mary had never yet been in school. Father and mother, when admonished of their duty, had always pretended that the child was too unwell to be at the time sent to school; and the frequency with which their residence in town had been changed, rendered it difficult for the authorities to take proper oversight of the children.

Mary was now in her own street, walking silently on, trying and trying whether the dear name which she had dreamed would not come back again.

With a friendly "Good evening, my child," a man in a black dress and white bands placed himself beside her. He had just been dispensing comfort at a dying bed.

Mary, buried in thought, was rather startled at the salutation, and stared with great eyes at the stranger, but did not recognise him, for she had never been in church, or only by accident for a few hasty moments. She returned laconically the hearty greeting, fell back again into the train of her meditations, and continued to proceed silently along the street.

The man, however, did not leave her, but entered into conversation, asking from what place she came so late, who her parents were, and in what state matters were at home; and as he spoke so affectionately and paternally, the child gradually opened her whole heart, and went on to tell of their great poverty, and how her mother was so sick, and her little brother and sisters hungered, and her father--but, as she mentioned her father, the tears started to her eyes, and she could not utter one word more for sobbing.

Then the pastor told her--for we already know that it was he--to keep up her spirits, and be of good cheer, better times might come round again. "For," said he, "there lives one, a good, rich, powerful Lord; they only required to apply to Him, and complain to Him of their want, and He would certainly help them; He had already assisted many thousands of poor people."

When the maiden heard these words, she suddenly stood still in the middle of the street, and the look with which she regarded the pastor distinctly asked, "Who is the Great Helper? Mention His name!" And the latter continued his discourse thus: "Do you not know the dear Lord who feeds the birds in the air, which sow not neither reap, and who clothes the lilies of the field, which toil not, neither spin, and yet are more beautifully arrayed than Solomon in all his glory? You surely know Him; or did you never hear of Jesus, the merciful Saviour?"

At these words Mary knew not what to make of it. Ah, thought she, transported with joy, now I have it! Yes! yes! so sounded the name which the birds in the wood praised in my dream!

She thought, but kept close all that had happened to her, and what she had met with, and said, in a touchingly suppliant voice, "Dear sir, tell me more of this Jesus;" and how willingly her friendly companion complied with her request!

He commenced and explained how all the children of men must have perished on account of their sins, had the great and holy God strictly and righteously dealt with them. He next told her of the merciful love of the Almighty--that it was so great that He rather gave for them His most beloved and eternal Son, than leave them to the destruction which they had deserved. This Son, though beyond all measure rich, yet for our sakes became a poor man and our brother, and is rightly named Jesus the Saviour. He staked His all to deliver us and redeem our lost inheritance; and He is now the helping friend of poor sinners, who still, though unseen, goes about over the land, and blessing, and dispensing kindness and comforts wherever He is but desired.

This was the substance of the discourse which the pastor held with the little wood-gatherer, in a way which children could understand.

Meanwhile, to the no small disappointment of the latter, they had reached the town. The pastor made the girl show him the dwelling of her parents, and, after again pressing her not to forget what she had heard, shook hands with her, and, with a hearty "Good night, my dear," took his departure. The girl returned the greeting from the bottom of her heart, thanked him for his words, and went on her way with the bundle of sticks. She had never gone there so light, so free, so happy as at this hour.

When she came home, her father was sitting behind the empty table, gloomy and silent, with his head resting on both hands. The mother was lying in her sick-bed, with immeasurable sorrow imprinted on every feature.

"What have you brought?" shouted the father, with a rigid face, as she entered.

"This wood, father," replied Mary; "and," added she, her countenance lighted up with joy, "a dear, dear friend, who has everything in abundance."

"A friend!" muttered the father; "what sort of friend is it, Mary?"

"One so powerful and rich, that it is an easy thing for him, dear mother, to restore you to health with a word, and no less quickly to bring you work, dear father, and all that we need."

"And this friend may be?"

"He is called Jesus, and"----

She would have said more, but scarcely had she pronounced the name Jesus than her father, with wild blasphemy and cursing, commanded instant silence, and threatened her with blows should she ever again think of coming to him with such fooleries and pronouncing that name.

And, alas! the sick mother was of the same opinion, and manifested as much anger as her husband, and said: "Had you brought us home a few pence for bread, that would have been better."

It is scarcely in the power of words to express what Mary felt at this reception. The weight upon her breast prevented her from uttering a single word more. She stole softly into the dark closet which was the common sleeping apartment of herself, her father, and two sisters.

Overcome with grief, she sank down on the hard straw mattress; and who knows whether she had ever again risen from it, had her oppressed heart not found relief in giving vent to a flood of clear tears, and had she not, at the same time, recalled to memory the kind, comforting form which had appeared to her in the dream.

"Oh, Lord Jesus," sighed Mary, "thou dear friend of poor sinners, see, see, how I also am a poor, poor, little bird; and my sisters, and we all, all! Oh, help us also! Restore my mother to health, and make my father cheerful and good! Give us bread, and peace; give us peace, and make us love Thee, and be obedient to Thee!"

Sobbing, she sighed it up, and sighed and whispered much more besides. Then she became still, and wept no more, for it was with her as if one sweet yes after another sounded in her ear. Full of blessed peace, she fell asleep. Hope was the good angel that closed her eyes.

Next morning she was the first out of bed, and cheerfully and actively busied herself in sweeping the room, and, as far as possible, putting everything in its place.

She then sat down by the bedside of her mother, and said, "Mother, certainly the Saviour helps!"

To her mother's question how she had fallen into this strange way of speaking, Mary began to relate all the occurrences of the day before,--how she had fallen asleep in the wood, what a dream she had had, how a well-disposed man had made up to her on the way, and this and that which he had spoken.

And she told it so lively, and with such simple and childlike gladness, that the mother could not be satisfied with hearing; and at length tears stood in her eyes, and she seized Mary's hand, and said, "Oh, Mary, that you would but dream once more!"

Meanwhile, the father also had entered the room; but when he heard the words, "Jesus," and "prayer," and remarked the solemn and impressed air of both mother and daughter, he broke into a fury, and said, "Mary, bring once more that absurd stuff to light, and you may look about for where to live; I tolerate you no longer here! Go and get bread. If matters do not soon take a different turn in my family, I am resolute, and there is nothing of which I will not be capable. The criminals in the penitentiary may be called happy compared with us, and death is to be preferred to this life of starvation and distress!"

He said this with a countenance of deep despair and a horrible aspect. Mary sprang towards him, clung tenderly to his knee, and said with a voice which might have moved a stone--

"Oh, father, do not be so sad, do not be so angry. You will see that we will certainly be helped!"

The father put her away from him, though with a gentle push; and, whether his heart was touched I know not, went in silence out of the room, shut the door behind him, and was soon lost in the streets of the town.

When he returned towards noon, sulky and out of humour, he found Mary busy, spreading a tattered napkin on the table, and laying earthenware dishes. At the same time she set as many knives and forks as could be found; and did it all with such a cheerfulness of her own, as if she was preparing for a feast anticipated by no one else.

"Have we anything to eat?" asked he.

"I do not understand either," chimed in the mother, "what the foolish child means."

Mary, however, rejoined, "I think some one will indeed provide something for us."

"Don't begin again to be absurd," shouted the father, and held his clenched fist close to the child's face.

Mary bent her head and was silent. Did she perhaps know some secret? She knew none; only her heart said, "The friend that feeds the birds cannot and will not forsake us!"

Just as it struck mid-day in the clock on the tower, the room-door, opened, and a neat, well-clad maid entered, with a great, and to appearance heavily-laden basket on her arm.

"My master's compliments," began she, "and you would perhaps accept this from him if you can use it. Mr. B. bids me say that you were so much in his mind last night, that he could scarcely sleep on your account. He then thought that you might possibly be in present difficulties; and should it be the case, you would perhaps excuse his sending this small contribution to your household. He will himself, in the course of a few days, come and see how matters stand with you."

Saying this, she emptied the basket, laid several beautiful loaves upon the table, handed forth a pot of butter, and a large piece of meat. There also lay at the bottom of the basket a cloth dress already worn, but still in good condition, and a piece of linen lay beside it. The maid said, "For shifts for the children."

When the shoemaker B. saw the one unpacked after the other, he stood like a pillar, and strove to utter a word of thanks, but was wholly unable. His wife made no less effort to stammer out from her sick-bed some expression of gratitude; but, as she would speak, she broke into loud sobbing, and instead of words, poured forth a stream of tears. Nothing remained but that little Mary should be the mouth of her parents.

"Give your good master," said the girl, "thousand, thousand thanks. The Lord Jesus will recompense what he has done for us in His name!" She then turned to her father and mother with joy beaming from her eyes, and said, "Do you see? there is indeed the dear, powerful Friend! Come let us eat what he has provided, and let us be happy!"

But hunger and thirst had left the parents. The father wept, standing speechless and as if thunderstruck in the middle of the room; then all at once he took up his little daughter, pressed her to his heart, and turned up his eyes as if he would direct them to heaven; and how further the hardened man began to weep and sob is scarcely to be told.

The mother called from her bed one time after another, "It is the Lord! it is the Lord!" but more than this her excessive agitation prevented her from saying.

The scene of tears was still continuing when the door opened afresh, and introduced the gentleman himself who had just sent the provisions and clothing, a substantial merchant of that place.

At the sight of the weeping faces he started, and stopped at the threshold, saying "Children, what is the matter with you?" No answer. "But I entreat you," continued he with increasing interest, "what has happened to you?"

Again no answer, but only a smile and a sigh through tears.

Then Mary took up the word once more, and said, "Dear, noble sir, it is from joy and gratitude that we are all weeping."

"Indeed," rejoined the benefactor, "that is well worth such a trifle. You see, Mr. B., I had to leave you two years ago, and give the work for my family to others, for, to tell you candidly, it was impossible to be any longer satisfied with you. I learned, besides, that you had entered upon an irregular life. I confess that since then I thought no more of you, until in the past night, as I could not sleep, all at once the thought of you entered my mind, and whether I would or not, I felt anxious for you. I should have hastened to you myself this morning had not an unforseen engagement thwarted my design; and in the meantime I forwarded the few refreshments. But now tell me how matters stand with you. That you were very poor I learned from those in my service, of whom I enquired this morning. Have you again bethought yourself of the duties which you owe wife and child? Just open up your heart to me, and explain all."

The master of the house stood a few seconds opposite his benevolent guest, with eyes fixed on the ground, and dumb; he then covered his face with his hands, and cried in a loud and truly heart-rending voice, "No, no! I am a godless man; but, with God's help"----

He would have said more, but tears choked his utterance.

His friendly visitor then grasped him by the right hand, and said, with winning kindness and gentleness, "Compose yourself, compose yourself; all may, all will take a turn for the better. Listen! Because I expect that you will henceforth lead a regular life, and keep steadily at your work, I will make an advance for the purchase of as much leather as you require, and not only will I give you the work from my house, but I hope to be able to procure other friends to do the same. Now, is that agreeable to you? Say what you think."

These words were scarcely pronounced, when the tradesman, deeply moved, suddenly fell upon his knees, and cried, "God be merciful to me a sinner! Mary, I now see it with my own eyes. Your Saviour lives!"

The mother, from her couch, made similar exclamations, and the generous guest kept ever and anon wiping his eyes.

At last he said, "Children, I pray you be still. You break my heart. Eat now; be cheerful. For to-day, farewell; I will return to-morrow." With this he left, moved to the very heart.

It would be tedious to relate in detail what further took place. From that time, in the cottage of the shoemaker, all old things passed away and all things became new. Those who had formerly been acquainted with the family no longer recognised it. Husband and wife walked hand and hand in the countenance of the Lord. Their union was of the happiest, their house a bright example to the whole neighbourhood. The children were trained up in the fear and admonition of the Lord, and, neatly clad, regularly attended the school of a pious teacher.

Mary bloomed in the society of the powerful and loving Friend who feeds the birds and clothes the lilies, happy and lovely as a flower of paradise in the dark valley of the earth. The father by and bye kept, sometimes three, sometimes even four journeymen, and his family had their daily bread in abundance.

He did not remain one farthing in the debt of his benefactor, who afterwards learnt, of course, all that had transpired previously to his first visit. He was even able to give something of his own to the treasury of love, and many a contribution for missionary, Bible, and other Christian associations, were received from him by the pastor, who kept the promise he had made to Mary of visiting them, and in no family of his parish passed his time oftener, or with greater pleasure, than in that of the shoemaker. The peace of God was enthroned beneath the richly blessed roof, for the Prince of Peace Himself had in mercy taken up His abode there.

The parents, afterwards, following close on each other, died in a joyful faith in Him who, in a twofold sense, had been to them resurrection and life.

Mary had been shortly before married to a cabinetmaker, an upright man, who was well aware what a pearl the Lord had presented him with in his wife. On the marriage day, the bridegroom made his bride a present of a beautiful family Bible, with gilt edges and silver clasps. The bride, in return, gave him a piece of embroidery, wrought by her own hand, and set in a gilt frame. There were on it full-topped trees, and branches decorated with all kinds of little birds. A kind form wandered beneath the shade of the trees, and strewed corn right and left for the happy songsters. At the foot of the piece, composed of particles of gold, might be read the words:--"Behold the fowls of the air: for they sow not, neither do they reap, nor gather into barns; yet your heavenly Father feedeth them. *Are ye not much better than they?*"

* * * * * * * *

Milton Keynes UK
Ingram Content Group UK Ltd.
UKHW012314040624
443649UK00007B/636